IAN MACMILLAN

THE SEVEN ORCHIDS

IAN MACMILLAN

THE SEVEN ORCHIDS

ISBN 0-910043-73-6

This is issue #88 (Fall 2005) of *Bamboo Ridge, Journal of Hawai'i Literature and Arts* (ISSN 0733-0308).

Published by Bamboo Ridge Press
Printed in the United States of America
Indexed in the American Humanities Index
Bamboo Ridge Press is a member of the Council of Literary Magazines and Presses (CLMP).

Cover and title page: *Moth Series: Number Seven,* by John Wisnosky
Photo of author and back cover photo: Susan Bates
Typesetting and design: Wayne Kawamoto

Bamboo Ridge Press is a nonprofit, tax-exempt corporation formed in 1978 to foster the appreciation, understanding, and creation of literary, visual, or performing arts by, for, or about Hawai'i's people. This project was supported in part by grants from the National Endowment for the Arts (NEA) and the State Foundation on Culture and the Arts (SFCA), celebrating over thirty years of culture and the arts in Hawai'i. The SFCA is funded by appropriations from the Hawai'i State Legislature and by grants from the NEA.

NATIONAL
ENDOWMENT
FOR THE ARTS

Bamboo Ridge is published twice a year. For subscription information, back issues, or a catalog, please contact:

Bamboo Ridge Press
P.O. Box 61781
Honolulu, HI 96839-1781
(808) 626-1481
brinfo@bambooridge.com
www.bambooridge.com

5 4 3 2 1   05 06 07 08 09

for Susan, Julia, and Laura

The large shed behind the sagging, termite-eaten house was in the process of falling in on the mountain of junk that it held, sheets of its rusted corrugated roofing slapping and bonging in the wind. Danielle Baker and her brother Kimo stood in the high weeds off to the side of the dirt driveway looking at the damaged roof, and then around at the windy landscape. The parched, grassy foothills above the town of Kaunakakai baked in the mid-morning heat, the wind steady from the east, and those flapping pieces of roofing had kept Danielle awake half the night. The metallic bonging sounds had been random, on and off, with long silent stretches that would be broken by a sudden, rapid slapping, so in the morning she had asked Kimo to help her nail it down. It occurred to her that she hadn't been out on this back section of the property since the first time she'd seen it.

"'Kay," she said. "Let's silence that mother."

"Can't hammer um," he said. "Buggah fall down."

"What'd you say Dad paid for this mess?"

"Two-fifty, but it's the land that's worth the money, not the house."

"If you want to go back to nature, why not go camping? Sometimes I wonder about him."

They made their way through the tall, parched weeds toward the structure. To their left, down the slope about fifty yards, was another house and barnlike structure, and sometimes during the day she saw an old woman outside watering flowers or hunched down in a squat pulling weeds from the lawn. She had been told that the woman was a longtime neighbor of the family her father had bought the property from. That lawn surrounding the house, and the structure behind the house, were clean and well kept, unlike the eyesore they approached. The entryway to the ruined shed was clear, and inside, just out of the sun, she saw that the dusty four-by-fours were off angle and the beams leading up to the hip part were cobwebbed and sagging, some sporting dusty abandoned birds' nests, lines of white, petrified droppings on the crossbeams underneath. Beyond the clear area was nothing but junk: flowerpots, bags of manure, and old pieces of wood piled so high that there was no clear way to get to the back of the interior, where, it appeared, parts of the roof were gone so that the sun slanted down in a plane that swirled with dust. There were what looked like flowers back there, the points of color just peeking over all the junk. Off to the left side sat an old green truck, without tires, its rusted wheels sunk down in the red dirt, the windows hazed over and bleached into the dull iridescence of greens and purples, its bed piled high with more flowerpots and rusted garden tools. "It's useless," she whispered. "We can't nail anything down. This whole thing is falling apart."

"Eh, why you whispering?" Kimo asked.

"Because get ghoses in here 'ass why," she said. She had been imitating Kimo's pidgin since they were kids, and even though he lapsed into it less frequently in his adulthood, she sometimes jumped on it when he did. But he didn't laugh. He snorted and looked around, then at her.

"So how do you feel?"

"Like a lower form of life, let's say a marsupial. Or a sea slug maybe. But I'll be all right."

The question made her picture the flask of gin she kept under the bed in her room, the little cushion that she had put in her suitcase before coming down to Moloka'i, from which she took tiny sips when it got too rough for her, and now, because he had asked the question, she wanted to go back and take just a little.

Kimo moved further into the mess, looking up as if expecting the roof to collapse while he was under it. "We get time," he said, "an' we clean this mess up. Make Dad's day ah? And the truck—is one fifty-one or -two International? Can restore um."

"Now there's something I'd like to do," Danielle said, and snorted. "Restore a truck." She followed, curious about the flowers she thought she saw in the back of the building. Where the sun slanted through the open roof, so much junk was piled up that she could no longer see what she had thought were the flowers. Kimo wedged himself between two mountains of bagged horse manure and potting soil, the plastic of the bags with their red writing oxidized to a faint pink, rotted and falling away from the pillow-forms of the manure and soil they had held. Surely this was a rats' mini-city, a centipedes' gathering place. Danielle followed Kimo, and once past the manure, she saw the flowers again, a line of them rising above all the crap, orchid plants that were so dehydrated that their tangles of worm-like gray roots appeared hollow, draped over large clay pots, and their leaves were brown and gray but for little live sections of green curving upward on the tops, from which sprouted spikes of buds, the lower ones opening, purple, yellow, orange, even one that appeared to be blue-green. They made a line across the back of the structure, and were placed, it appeared, on some sort of a wooden shelf, spaced a few feet apart, their roots glued to the wood. Kimo had moved to her right, to study the roof at the corner of the structure, and she wedged herself between some old wooden pallets and reached out to steady herself on the orchid shelf, and when she put her hand on it, she found that it was a thick board that was vertical instead of a shelf, and the unexpected feeling of having her fingers close over the inch-thick board startled her for a moment so that she lost her balance and her hand slid to the right and caught a splinter, right in the palm. The pain raced up her arm, and she had to slide her hand back to the left to get it off the thick splinter. She stumbled back over the pallets and into an open space. "Shit," she said.

"What?"

"Nothing. I cut myself."

She held her hand up in a fist, her middle fingertip jammed down on the hole in her palm, and then looked at it. The blue-edged hole leaked blood down over the heel of her hand, and a single line of it made its way down her wrist, very dense in color, in the darkness looking almost purplish-black. "Shit," she said.

"Lemme see," Kimo said. She held her hand out, shaking, and he held it and looked at the wound. "Let it bleed a little. No wan' dakine. What? Tetanus?"

"It's all right," she said. She stared at the line of blood on her wrist. "I'll go wash it and—" She continued staring at the line. "Shit. So now my only recreation is taken away."

"Wrap it up good an' tight. You can still paddle."

She envisioned the grassy section of Kaunakakai waterfront, where, late every day or two, she met with friends of hers, and they went out on one-man and two-man outrigger canoes, a little armada of misfits who thought they were practicing for the channel race and knew at the same time that most of them weren't going, because the club they belonged to wasn't really a club and the one they were sup-posed to join with for the race was on Maui. She and the other rejects were low on the list of those who would be permitted to go. Two or three of them maybe.

"Doesn't make any difference anyway," she said. "It's just a little exercise, nothing important."

Her father had bought the property three months earlier, fueled by some romantic dream of raising flowers for a living as a means of dealing with a divorce from his second wife, or at least following some slightly less romantic dream of fixing the old place up and selling it at a profit. But he rarely went to it. There was an old rotary phone in the kitchen, whose pink Formica counter was worn down in the middle to a dull white, and the only TV they had was Kimo's little one with a VCR that they sometimes used to watch rented movies. Danielle and Kimo went to the old place on the weekends they had free, Kimo because he had surf friends there, herself because Mark, her boyfriend, sometimes had to go to L.A. on weekends, and that was how Danielle met the friends she now had. Kimo was Danielle's half-brother, her own mother having died when she was four. She had often thought that the death of her mother might be something that had screwed her up, but realized also that she could barely remember her. She had seen pictures, and had noted with no more than a kind of dull academic interest how she resembled the woman in the pictures, the light brown hair and the lanky, even marginally athletic body-style, but any feeling of loss she might have felt was buried too far in the past for her to even wonder about the woman. Her stepmother, a hapa local from Maui, had Kimo right around the time she married Danielle's father.

In the bathroom of the old house, she ran water over the wound and squeezed blood out until it seemed clean enough, and then poured peroxide on the hole, riding out the sting and watching it bubble up into an off-white foam. All the time she did this her hand shook, not from the pain but because of the feeling of irritation in her flesh. She thought of herself as banished here, mostly her father's doing. She had lost her job, had blown almost all her money having fun, and had come close to blowing her health too. She had been living in Makiki with Mark, a haole from California she had assumed was simply independently wealthy, until she found out that his wealth came from selling drugs, not street-corner stuff but distribution, which, when she had originally considered it, didn't seem like pushing. It was more like a business that a lot of people in Hawai'i were in. It was really safe, he told her, and nothing for her to be concerned about. She had agreed with what he said, because after all, he was thirty-four and knew what he was doing. "It's a business," he had said, "and stupid as it sounds, it pumps life into the economy. The fact that it's illegal is really a small matter. There's dealing everywhere you look out here. That's just the way it is. Every neighborhood has somebody cooking meth, and the smell of acetone is as familiar as the smell of plumeria." It had worried her a little, especially when she thought of the idea of her complicity, should he ever be caught. But the nightlife was too attractive to her to make that information about him significant enough to change anything. She had worked as a receptionist in a car dealership and had begun falling asleep at her desk. Her boss called her in one day and told her that she was a sweet girl and lots of fun too but he had a business to run, and so she was let go. It didn't bother her. Because Mark had money, she ended up being able to save some of her own.

She had a little bit of her own life and a few friends outside of Mark's life and his friends, and that was paddling, and the people she knew from her club. The exercise, she thought, balanced off the effects of the alcohol, so the late spring practice and the beginning of the regatta season occupied enough of her energy that she assumed that the perfect balance had been struck, vigorous exercise in the afternoon, the nightlife after that, and without a job it had seemed to her almost perfect.

But there were signs, she had known even then, that things were out of hand and out of her control—one morning she woke up, got out of the bed in which Mark was snoring, and tiptoed toward the bathroom, and stopped. Sleeping on the couch was a blonde, middle-aged woman, and leaning against the couch was a wheel from a mountain bike. She went back and woke Mark up, whispered that a strange woman was sleeping in the living room. Mark had said, "Oh, that's Shirley. You met her last night." Shirley? She could not remember having met any Shirley the previous night, nor could she remember anything beyond eating dinner at a restaurant whose name she couldn't remember.

Then she had wondered what had happened when they'd returned to the apartment. She stumbled to the bathroom and looked for evidence that there had been something, well, kinky going on, but when she concentrated on herself, she realized that her body, her skin, told her that nothing had happened. When she was finished using the bathroom she tiptoed past the woman named Shirley and into the kitchen, where she downed a gulp of scotch, and when that didn't help her recall a single detail from the previous night, that is, after they ate dinner, she had another.

Shirley had left sometime later, as Danielle slept. When it came time for Mark to explain Shirley, he said, "Oh, she's a homeless woman I know." And the bike tire? "She stole that," Mark told her. When Danielle asked him why the woman would steal a bike tire, he laughed. "We were drunk," he said. "She said that you never know when a bike tire'll come in handy. In fact, you advised her to take it to the swap meet." Amazingly, the eccentric homeless lady had taken the tire with her when she had left. Danielle finally thought that the weird episode was simply funny, and no more. She thought that the phone calls she heard Mark make, his voice sometimes demanding and tough, sometimes almost obsequious, were just phone calls, none of her business. His odd hours were none of her business. The answer was always to keep the wool over her eyes and have fun.

Another sign came when she was driving one morning over the Pali to go to the beach with a friend she had met at a club, a girl she had known from high school who convinced her to come over for a visit. She was going up the road toward the tunnels and lapsed into a bright nightmare in which she did not know who she was or where she was going or why she was in this thing she could not identify as a car. She felt as if she were nothing but a pair of floating eyes, locked into some awed fascination at what she saw and felt: trees sweeping by and out of her vision, and forward motion, the strange hum and vibration of whatever she was sitting in, her hands locked on a circle that she could not identify as a steering wheel. She continued moving forward, waiting for something to come to her mind that might tell her who or what she was, but nothing came, and she remained locked in that fascination with the horrible, senseless brightness of everything she saw. When whatever she was in entered the darkness of the tunnel, she re-emerged from that dream, breathless and frightened, because she could easily have turned the wheel and aimed with that same awed fascination at a tree or oncoming truck. She had to concentrate on driving the rest of the way as if she were now just learning to drive. By the time she had reached her friend's house, she had passed it all off as nothing more than a phase of some remnant alcohol flash.

She kept up with the clubbing and having fun until one day she was so sick that she vowed to change herself. But that lasted only until the sun went down, and she woke up the next day feeling the same as the day before, but for one difference: she had low back pain and had to go to the bathroom every five or ten minutes, and became so aggravated by a full day of this that she went to a doctor, who told her with a straight-faced objectivity that she was experiencing a case of temporary kidney damage, and that if she continued, she risked far more than an overactive bladder. Her response to that was to do the same thing that landed her in the doctor's office, and she noted the next day, with a sort of musing wonder, her head pounding and her mouth dry and her hands shaking, that she had that same overactive bladder, and almost as if the obvious had become too mysterious for her to comprehend, she waited patiently until the night came and went on doing the same thing, until after a few days of it she went to her father's house and in a conversation admitted to him, imitating the doctor's studious objectivity, what was wrong with her.

Her father was a calm, nice man, always had been, but the look on his face this time was not the look he had once gotten when she had misbehaved in high school, or crumpled a fender of the car. He was half angry and half shocked, and told her that she was in trouble, probably had been for longer than even she knew, and that she would either straighten herself out or risk losing her family, too. Her friend Mark, he told her, was probably the worst influence she could have, because he stood as a kind of validation of everything self-destructive she was doing. You're twenty-four, he said, and I can't tell you what to do, but right now I'm telling you what to do, see? She agreed with all of this, saying, yes, you're right. What should I do? Tell me what to do. He said that she had to separate herself from these people, she had to get away from all the shit that had sucked her in, and she had flinched at that because he never used language like that to her before. The only thing that he thought was 'interesting' about all this was that she was not on drugs. She had tried some of them and had not liked the reaction, the warped perception in which the world seemed to her like some dizzying cartoon. But she had never developed a problem with drugs like so many of her friends, some of whom, she realized with that same musing confusion that she felt when she looked carefully at herself, some of whom were already dead. Wasn't that interesting, that some of her high school friends were already dead? Well, her father said, you don't have to follow them if you don't want to. I don't really think I want to, she told him after thinking about it for a few seconds, as if it were a question that required careful consideration. No, I don't think I want to do that. Tell me what to do.

He described the beauty and serenity of Moloka'i, and she said, yes, I know that, I go there on weekends sometimes. Kimo would be down there, at least until the University kicked off the fall semester, so she'd have company. He explained to her what he wanted to do with this new property. He couldn't do it himself now, and thought of it as a down-the-road kind of thing, where one day he would retire, to raise something, flowers, whatever, he didn't care. The spectacular natural beauty and the legendary serenity of Moloka'i frightened her, not so much because of the isolation but because of the boredom she knew she would have to endure, a boredom so exaggerated that it seemed as if it might be terminal. Spectacular natural beauty in general bored her. After all, she had grown up here, and she looked at mountains and ocean and beautiful greenery with no more than a dull-eyed objectivity. For Christ's sake, that stuff's been there since the day I was born. Sometimes, at the beach, her brother would stare off at the ocean, or the sea-cliffs, and then say to her, Jesus, this is beautiful, and she would say, yeah, it really is, and then walk off a little confused that she was unable to see in the scenery what Kimo saw.

She moved out of the apartment she shared with Mark. She explained to him all that her father had explained to her, and he sat there with this very casual, passive look on his face and said, hey, whatever you need to do. You know I'm always here. And that was that. It was interesting, she had thought, that it was so easy, not so much for her but for Mark. It was as if she had meant so little to him that her moving out did not even seem to change his expression—hey, whatever you need to do. It's cool with me. So this, she thought, was love in America at the beginning of the new century. Hey, been nice to know you—keep in touch. During her last trip down the elevator she cried, because it was so easy for him, and she thought that some emotion should be felt by somebody. She put herself back together before the doors slid open on the ground floor.

Now that she had been here four days, subsisting on small amounts of gin and otherwise doing nothing but waiting for the afternoon so that she could meet the misfits at the beach, she had settled into a routine that she knew was vacant of anything good for her, and the boredom she had feared had now taken over to the point that she existed in a lazy fog, unable to make herself interested in anything. Remembering her reaction to taking the splinter in her hand, she thought, at least I don't add 'wimp' to the list of possible nicknames I could carry. She took care of the throbbing in the palm of her hand with an extra belt of gin. To pass the time until she would go, she spruced up her room and some of the downstairs rooms of the house, which her father had furnished with high-end Salvation Army furniture, including junk aluminum pots and pans for the kitchen to go with what was left from the original occupants, or in this case occupant, some old woman who had died. Her own room, upstairs and across a hall from Kimo's, was large enough, but nearly bare—an old bed, a heavy oak dresser, a half-rotted old rug and an ornately framed mirror on the wall. She understood that the bed and the dresser were there when her father had bought the place. The rest was dull yellow tongue and groove walls and a floor of warped planking that had grit in all the gaps between the planks. She needed to put up curtains, paint the floor, put something to look at on the walls, but these projects seemed somehow too complicated right now, and she did not have the energy to do it. She looked with a kind of swooning aggravation at the shabbiness of the whole house, the feeling made worse because she knew she could not generate the energy to do what she knew she should do.

Her friends carried a series of nicknames appropriate to their misfit status, and they had no shame about both admitting it and using the names on each other. It might have been the random nature of their meeting, but any pretense of superiority on the part of any one of them had been checked early on in a series of frank, confessional talks amongst themselves. There was something about Moloka'i that made possible a honesty that would not have been possible on O'ahu. Danielle drove the little rusty family Tercel down the hill toward Kaunakakai where they would meet, her hand tightly wrapped with a square of gauze and taped all the way around. The town was a dusty, seemingly accidental model of a western outpost town, with low buildings and grit in the wind, and usually its sidewalks were peopled by digital camera–toting tourists in their new aloha wear. The grocery and dry goods store, Misaki's, fit perfectly with its faded plastic signs, one of which read 'Tanya Will Tan-Ya Hawaiian.' Inside it was crowded and grubby by Honolulu standards, but she liked the ambience. As if to match the damaged, utilitarian quaintness of the town, the water all along the south facing shore was brown and a little murky from silt runoff, all the way out toward the east end, where, a few miles from the end of the island, it was clean and blue.

First, she would go to the Wines and Spirits store and buy another bottle of gin. Subsistence drinking was all right, she discovered, as long as you didn't interrupt it. How much she ended up peeing would be the standard.

Today she would be paddling with The Fat Lady, The Airheads, and The Basket-Case. Her partner in a two-man was The Basket-Case, a former investment counselor who had lost everything on dotcom stocks and certain risky investment strategies, had gone bankrupt, and was left now with a little cottage a few miles east of Kaunakakai and enough money to live without reducing herself to changing beds in one of the hotels. Her name was Donna Strong, and she had made a feeble attempt at suicide eight months earlier with a bottle of sleeping pills, was forty years old, and went around with a fixed expression of something combining surprise, awe, and a kind of muddled distance from everything, as if she had just awakened and discovered that there was a huge party going on and she had been overlooked in the invitations. That estranged look, along with the business of a suicide attempt, didn't seem to match—she was young-looking for forty, tall, and in good shape, dark brown hair unblemished by even one gray hair. And she had a son who was nineteen, off on the mainland in college—she had plenty to appreciate. Danielle suspected that she was a victim of clinical depression or some other syndrome, because of the way she could remain distant and sour for no apparent reason.

The Fat Lady was Marcia Soares, a local girl thirty years old, who liked to flirt and was obsessed with losing weight and could not be convinced that mochiko chicken bentos might be part of her problem. The Airheads were Chrissy Moore and Michelle Forten, California girls from Kīhei, who came to Molokaʻi because they thought it was cool to try living in a place so dead and remote, and like, they thought the natural beauty of the place was like just so way out there. They were somewhat famous for showing up at regatta races on Maui with perfect makeup and jewelry, as if kidnapped from a cool party, and decked out in their skin-tight racing threads. One oddity about them was that Chrissy Moore came from a family of eight foster children, was reared in a tiny village in northern California, and was effectively penniless. She had one natural older sister among all her foster siblings. Her parents had been victims of drug problems and had left the two girls, ages three and five, with their grandmother who had been unable to take care of them. Chrissy was awed by her own liberation from the boonies, and had learned the complicated bearing of the valley girl airhead from Michelle Forten, who came from, of all places, Beverly Hills. They looked like sisters, and the compensation for the difference in their backgrounds was Michelle's financial assistance, which was, like, no problem for her. They had laughed at themselves, and Michelle even said, "I know, I know, like, I'm what you would call a bimbo. An airhead." Chrissy Moore seconded that by saying, "One of these days we'll like, grow up already, but you know, being a bimbo is fun." They worked at the Kaluako'i Hotel.

Then there was The Poet, Tricia Nakamoto, an attractive little girl who wrote poetry and had once wanted to become a famous Asian-American writer, but was so hopelessly shy that she could never read anything she wrote to an audience, much less develop the confidence to send something to a magazine with publication in mind. She had one irritating habit: the way she looked at people. Danielle would catch Tricia looking at her sometimes, almost as if Danielle were some fascinating display or some strange life form to be studied by a scientist. Whenever something made her laugh, she would produce a soft giggle and then cut it off, as if momentarily doubtful about the sound of her own voice. She also had this weird habit of whispering to herself, her face held in a closed-in attention to whatever it was she whispered, as if she were always accompanied by some ghost, or invented companion. She had already graduated from the University, and was back home, keeping in touch by e-mail with one of her professors who was a poet and her 'mentor' as she called the woman.

Missing from the roster today was Judy Beeman, who might be called The Recluse because of her tendency toward secrecy about her phone number and her refusal to have a credit card, but she was dubbed The Barf Queen. She wanted nothing more than to do the channel race, but could not get a hundred yards out into the lagoon at Kaunakakai without feeding her lunch to the fish, because she did not believe in taking medicines that prevented seasickness, this conviction a spin-off of some bizarre 'you're your own problem' pop-psychology thing she could not shake. She said that ginger was the only thing that would work for her, and it didn't. She looked like a dowdy refugee from the '60s, and was proud of not having taken an aspirin in nearly twenty years, and often diagnosed others by saying that the problem was that their bodies were full of stored toxins (which made Danielle briefly flush, because Judy was probably right on target where it applied to her). She would not live in Honolulu because it was rife with toxins, and Maui was almost as bad. And she would not live in Honolulu because her former husband was there, a man who had beaten her and against whom she'd had numerous restraining orders. Was he a hippie too? Tricia Nakamoto had asked, because she thought hippies were supposed to be peace-loving people. Not when they're on LSD, Judy Beeman had said. And when you have a superiority complex and take LSD, you become very difficult to live with.

And by her own admission to the others, Danielle was The Drunk, simplified from the more elaborate nicknames that might have been bestowed upon her: AA Case, Miss Eighty-eight Proof, or her favorite, bestowed upon her one afternoon at the beach by Tricia Nakamoto, a title this time preceded by the strange little giggle: The Queen of the Sunrise Headache.

She parked the Tercel under a tree and saw them down at the water by their canoes. Chrissy Moore and The Poet were already out on the water. Danielle broke the seal of the gin flask and took a small swig, just enough to steady her nerves, and reached behind her to pull out her paddle, that fifty-one inch piece of wood that had stayed with her through it all, re-varathaned fifty times over the years along the blade edges. It was the one possession she had that felt pure to her, without any taint or embarrassing history.

Donna Strong and Michelle Forten, the remaining Airhead, saw her approaching and waved, while The Fat Lady worked on screwing in the aluminum 'iakos of her rig. Despite the wind, the water looked calm, and there were no waves breaking against the long, concrete jetty that ran out to the edge of the bay. The high, green and reddish profile of Lānaʻi hung in a soft salt haze, a couple of white sails sweeping along the bottom.

"What happened to your hand?" Donna Strong called.

"Cut it," she said. "No problem though. It's in the palm so I can still paddle."

"So where are we going?" Michelle Forten asked.

"Let's try Kakahaia Park, or whatever that's called." It was a few miles east of Kaunakakai, a narrow stretch of picnic area where the shoreline was calm and they could get out and rest.

Michelle Forten stared at the water. "But like is this the way to get ready? Aren't we supposed to be all battling the swells? Practicing steering? Every day I'm all, 'when are we gonna do the cool stuff?' and we go along the shoreline to a picnic area. I mean wow, is that rigorous or what?"

"We practice this way until we get the Force-Five," Donna Strong said. "If they're inclined to give us the Force-Five, that is. I can't get much out of the coach."

Michelle shook her head. "You know, we have to screw with our schedules for this. Chrissy has to like agonize over the hours she loses. I think the coach should put up or shut up."

"No, he likes to tease, you know, suggest and imply and do things with his eyes, so he can feel a kind of fulfillment when he sees us holding our breaths before he tells us who gets the shaft."

Michelle snorted and folded her hands under her chin. "Ple-ease," she squeaked.

"Yeah, that's about right," Donna said. "Learn how to grovel. This helps make his day." Michelle snorted again and turned to look out at Chrissy and The Poet.

Donna turned to Danielle. "Everything I used to own is still taking it on the chin," she said. "Can you believe that?"

"I wouldn't even look it up," Danielle said.

"I know, I know," she said. "It's just interesting. It would've been seven hundred fifty thou I lost instead of a measly six hundred. It's fascinating. If I'd stayed in it a week longer I'd be living in the park, my stuff in a grocery cart."

"So with the Force-Five," Michelle said, turning back to them, "we might be like, out of it, is what you're saying, right? Like, 'sorry girls, it's no go'."

Marcia Soares looked up from her work. "Eh," she said. "Dis not over until I sing, 'kay?"

The three of them standing above Marcia looked in confusion at each other.

"Until I sing," Marcia said. "Come on—yoa brains no work?"

Donna snorted. "Okay okay, I got it, but it's lame," she said, and to Danielle and Michelle, she said, "until the fat lady sings?" Danielle laughed, thinking at the same time that Marcia shouldn't poke fun at herself that way—she wasn't that fat, she was simply tubular and a little substantial in the rear end. Where she was supposed to narrow at the waist she did not. Otherwise she might be thought of as simply 'hefty'.

Marcia stood up and arched her back, then looked at Danielle's hand. "Can do um?"

"It's no problem," she said. With that statement, she felt a little surge of adrenaline, as if here there was one thing that made existing worthwhile.

She discovered that she was right about the paddle—the placement of the wound was such that it made almost no contact with the rounded paddle handle, and when they were almost to the end of the jetty and open water, Danielle was aware that whatever exhilaration she should have felt wasn't there. It was paddling, that was all, a means of getting from here to there, the gin having leveled everything out, to the point that she didn't know what the reason was for anything she did.

She had bad dreams. The consistent throbbing in the palm of her hand radiated up her arm, and in the middle of the night she heard a cacophony of sounds: the rapping of corrugated metal sheeting in the wind, voices overlapping to the point that there was no space of silence between statements, and she was aware of parched orchids baking in the heat, and she woke up once sweating because the wind had died away for a while and left the air hot and still. When she slept again the voices returned, and she saw an old woman walking along a rusted chain-link fence on the other side of which was the ocean, and the woman walked and walked, her eyes always on the water, and her face was creased with a musing ageless smile aimed at that water, and she walked and walked, the rags she wore flapping in the wind, always smiling as if she expected the fence to have a gate in it but there was no gate and she kept on walking, and walked for years with that smile on her face always looking at the water which lapped up on the sand just fifty feet from the rusted chain-link fence that had no gate.

When she woke up she thought that the woman she had dreamt of must have been the one from the place next door. Or if not that lady, maybe she had dreamt of herself walking in some arid landscape where there was no access to alcohol. She heard the refrigerator door thump shut downstairs, and then Kimo dragging a chair on the bare floor. He would be gone in five minutes, off to surf. Her hand no longer throbbed, but it felt tender, and she peeled away the bandage she had put on it after paddling practice and looked at the hole. It was not fringed with red, which probably meant that it was healing nicely. To get herself off the ground, she reached under her bed and grabbed the gin bottle, and pulled it along the gritty floor so that it produced a squeak that made her shudder. She poured a small glass one-third full of gin, and drank it, and then just as Kimo left, the screen door slapping behind him, she went downstairs and ate cereal and juice and a vitamin pill. As for making her way through the day, she decided first to drag the hose out and see if she could arc a stream of water over all the crap in the building and hit those orchids. It was easy enough to do, although it didn't seem like a good idea to soak all the bags of manure and the wood piled all over the place. She found a spigot on the side of the structure, attached the hose, and then made her way through the high weeds to the back corner of the building, where she could see the strange line of orchids at an angle, below them six-foot tall weed grasses that had grown up and pushed by the wind, leaned against the partly open backside of the building. Apparently that wall of the building had once had a line of windows, or a long opening of some kind. She stood there for a few minutes playing the water over the orchids, holding her thumb down as hard as she could to narrow and give distance to the stream of water, which, in the wind, carried all the way to the last orchid. How they had made it through the summer without drying up was a mystery to her, but watering them made her feel a little better.

After that there was nothing—Kimo would follow his surfing with fishing or hiking or something like that. He had a lot of friends. And soon, only a week and a half or a little more, Kimo would be in Honolulu. He might come back to Moloka'i some weekends and he might not. Then, she imagined, her isolation would be worse, along with the fear she had of staying in the house alone. So there was nothing but the passage of time, while she sat and thought, aware that this was the essence of her banishment from the lights of Waikīkī. Were she still there, she was sure that at the moment she would be waiting for the next trip to the bathroom, rubbing her low back where the pain was, and nursing a world-class headache with Tylenol and a bit of the hair of the dog. Mark would be perfectly happy, jovial and without any visible symptom of his excess, sitting there on the lanai reading

25

the paper and blurting out one interesting story or another: hey, the volleyball 'Bows are going up in the ranks; hey, we got another school shooting, this one in Texas. Shit, we can't do without at least one a week right? It's so American.

When she was finally released from the jail of nothing to do, she drove the Tercel down the hill to Kaunakakai to meet the girls, who were as usual milling around the canoes. Danielle would take The Poet's one-man so that The Poet could practice steering sitting behind The Basket-Case. The thought occurred to her that if a few of them did get to do the channel race and didn't have a good steersman, they would very likely huli the canoe four or five times, because nobody but Tricia was any good at steering, and one wrong move would flip the ama over. Danielle wanted to stroke, because she preferred having nothing but the front of the canoe before her, and she thought of herself as a slightly stronger paddler than the rest, not so much because the size of her upper body, which was routine, but because she thought she held her concentration better. Also, Marcia and Judy Beeman couldn't get in the canoe on open-ocean changes without hooking their legs over the gunnel, hence in paddling language they were called 'hookers'. Danielle had learned paddling as a child, and never forgot her first coach, who made the twelve-year-old girls memorize the three words: rhythm, balance, power. That was paddling. And she thought she was at the very least a decent paddler. The Airheads could be, but they would lose their concentration like for sure if like some group of guys with awesome bricks went sweeping by and they had to like wave at them and all, and The Basket-Case fatigued easily.

"You know," Donna Strong said as Danielle approached, "there won't be much point unless they get us the canoe. What are we supposed to do, line up three of these to make the forty-five feet? I mean, our reserve status means that there might be no reason to let us have one."

"Yeah, I know," she said. Then she waved at the others, who had turned when Donna Strong spoke. "We'll get it. We've still got more than a month."

Michelle Forten rose up from a one-man and said, "I think this affiliation thing sucks. It's like, 'wow, we forgot the Moloka'i girls.' And like when do we practice the changes? Is The Barf Queen ever showing? It's like, hey, today's the race, I think I better go down there. This sucks."

"I'll call her," Donna Strong said. "I'm her contact, and all I have to do is convince her that I'm not blowing her cover."

"Can she be that paranoid?"

"I guess," Donna said.

"And where will we stay in Waikīkī?"

Chrissy Moore, standing behind Michelle, winced.

"Who says we're staying?" Donna asked.

"I don't know about this," Chrissy said. "I mean—"

"We'll cover it," Michelle said.

"I'm gonna owe you my soul before this is over." Chrissy then got this look of a kind of thoughtful perplexity. "I have three older sisters already, even though two are of the foster type, and they floated me and gave me rides. It's not what I wanted out here. What I want—" She squinted into the distance somewhere past her listeners.

"Is?" Michelle asked.

"This is important," Danielle said. "It's what she wants out of life."

"What I want out of life," Chrissy said, "is a Toyota Tacoma."

They all laughed. "Well," Chrissy said, "you have to like start somewhere, right? So I want a truck."

"Why that one?" Danielle asked.

"Anything with more than two seats makes me nervous. Every day I ride in Michelle's Forester, and I'm thinking, I've got another sister giving me rides. I have not like, advanced yet."

"Okay, I understand," Danielle said. "But look, we need you. We'll chip in, call it a flat travel grant."

"Right," Donna said. "We'll call it an educational travel grant, to expose the hick to the lights of the big city."

"I've already seen those lights," Chrissy said, "and I've seen hotel bills too. You go out for a few drinks, then sleep in this room, and it costs like two hundred bucks."

"But it's Waikīkī," Michelle said.

Danielle thought about that. Waikīkī. But Chrissy was right. It would cost too much. "I'm coming back after the race," she said.

"If I no come back," Marcia Soares said, "I get lickens. Kids be in skoo den."

They got their canoes into the water. Danielle didn't really care anyway. Hanging out with the girls was enough—they didn't have to do a channel race to bond properly. They made their way out past the concrete jetty and into open water, and as usual, went toward the narrow strip of picnic area about six miles from Kaunakakai, where, as they made their way in, they saw a group of dark men lashing a blue and white Bradley.

They carried their canoes up onto the grass. The Airheads carried theirs with their heads aimed in the direction of the men. "That's Hui whatever, right? That club?"

Marcia Soares laughed. "You woa yoa junk clothes ah? Lef' yoa spandex at home? Bummers."

"See that guy at the end?" Chrissy whispered. "He works at the ranch. His name is Hayward, I think. He's sorta quiet but he's a cool guy."

"I think my brother knows him," Danielle said.

The Airheads fussed with their hair, turned their baseball caps backwards, and wandered down toward the men.

"Let us observe the beginning of the human mating ritual," Donna Strong said. "Watch carefully as the two females check out the unsuspecting studs surrounding their aquatic vessel."

"Yes," Danielle said. "One has spotted the females, as you can see. Obvious signals have begun to manifest themselves in his bearing. He appears both flustered and at the same time aroused."

"The females instantly understand the signs. They begin to sign back, if you will, with body language, their breath drawn in to expand their chests, as is observed in some birds. Ah, they speak."

"The conversation is routine, but fraught with subliminal messaging. Now two more of the males note their presence, and indeed, the numbering of this encounter is immediately apparent. Six as opposed to two. Their chests also expand. They become aware of posture and stand erect—I mean in posture—and steal glances at each other, carefully mapping out strategy in this competition for the attentions of these females, and so on."

"Enzymes and fluids begin to move. Pheromones float upon the air."

"Now look, one of the females has selected her prey, while the other, confused, experiences flashes of anxiety at this bounty of choice. And look—" They watched. "Yes, she now fiddles with her cap, deciding that the bill of the cap should be frontwards rather than backwards."

Donna Strong laughed. "Kids," she said.

While The Airheads talked with the guys, the remaining four sat in the grass in the shade, facing the high profile of Lāna'i. Gradually the group around the canoe drifted up into the shade, still talking, and Danielle got up and wandered down to the Bradley, wanting for some reason to be away from the voices of the others. She stopped near it, and then fell into an odd pause, as if she had just realized that she had forgotten something important. She stood there in a peculiar, hollow silence staring at the Bradley, wondering why she was doing that, what the point of wandering down here had been. She walked along the right side, peered over at the banana-shaped ama and the looped 'iakos, and put her hand out to touch the hull, then wrapped her fingers over it.

"My God," she whispered.

"What is that mess?" Donna asked. They made their way through the weeds behind the house, Danielle leading the way.

"It was like a barn or something. The people who owned it grew flowers. My dad's thinking of doing that."

"So what's the big mystery? What am I doing here?"

"I just wanted to check something out. I don't wanna go in there alone, that's all. If the roof caves in I want someone to know where to go to collect my dismal remains."

"And disposing of them?"

"Put them in a Hefty bag and lean them against the mailbox."

Donna laughed. They made their way to the opening, and Danielle looked for a way to get across, and changed her mind. "Let's go around back," she said. "C'mon, I'll show you."

"Rats," Donna said. "Centipedes. You go."

"No, it's just weeds." She looked down at her zoris. Donna was wearing them too. "Step lightly," she said.

At an oblique angle, at the back corner, they could see the line of orchids. Danielle began working her way through the weeds, stomping them down carefully, making sure there weren't boards with nails in them or broken glass.

"Who's that?" Donna whispered.

"Who's what?"

Donna tipped her head in the direction of the next place, and they saw the old woman doing something near the hedge. "Oh, that's our neighbor," Danielle said. "I haven't met her." Then the woman turned and went down toward her house. Danielle shrugged and worked on toward the orchids. The weeds there were tall grasses that had tassels, some of which were higher than the orchids. Danielle got to the third orchid in the line, and began pulling at the high grass, which was jammed in under the orchid pot. When it came away they saw the sun-bleached wood, the shellac peeling in thick sheets away from it, and the wood swept down and curved under. "Jesus," Danielle said. "Look." She pulled more weeds away, and there was no question—the rounded plank ran to the next orchid, and in a hole behind the high grasses they could see it sweep to the next one. She worked her way closer, feeling with her foot for a flat surface to stand on. She reached out and put her hand on the top of the plank. It was a full inch thick, as on the other side, where that splinter had caught the heel of her hand. "I'll bet it's koa," she said.

Donna looked along the canoe hull, then back. "What about the thingies, front and back?"

"The manus? They'd be—" She looked into the darkness of the building. "They'd be separate pieces, over there maybe." She pointed into one of the corners. There was no way to see what was there. She stepped back a little and ran her eyes along the line of orchids. "It's got to be thirty-five feet at least. There's an orchid for each seat, plus one."

"Why is it here?"

"I don't know."

Without looking away from the canoe, Donna said, "That old lady is back, and she's watching us."

Danielle turned. The old lady was at the hedge and peering over at them. Then she waved for them to come to the hedge. Just as she did so, Danielle saw Donna looking back in the other direction, and

31

turned to look—The Poet was standing at the corner of the shed, looking absurdly like a kid left out of some game. Danielle groaned, then
whispered, "What's *she* doing here?" and then felt badly about having
said that. Tricia stood there with a 'what is going on here?' look on
her face, and Donna pointed to the canoe, which she looked at until
Danielle said, "C'mon, let's see what the old lady wants."

Tricia made her way through the weeds, and then stopped once
she recognized what they had found. "Hey, that's a canoe," she said.

"Koa probably," Danielle said. "C'mon, let's meet our neighbor."

They made their way single-file through the high weeds toward
the hedge, which was topped and apparently squared off on the old
lady's side, but uncut on their side, so that the branches came out
from the bases of the shrubs ten or twelve feet. When they were close
enough to see clearly the friendly creased Japanese tutu face, the lady
smiled and held up a clear plastic box. "You my new neighbahs ah?
Come, I make cone sushi fo' you."

"Oh, thank you," Danielle said. "I can't reach though."

"No come down dis way. Get one hole inna hedge an' you can
come t'rough. Come come, I show you." She went on down the hedge,
to a place where some of the bushes were missing, and the three of
them made their way through and out onto a closely cut, very green
lawn. Danielle introduced Donna and Tricia to the old lady, and then
herself.

"I Mollie Teruya," the lady said, and handed Danielle the box of
sushi.

"Can we eat them now?" Tricia whispered, and then produced a
soft laugh that ended too early.

"Eat eat," Mollie Teruya said. "Dey da right tempatcha now."

Danielle opened the box. There were eight of the sushis inside,
and she took one out, as did Tricia and Donna.

"I see you wen' fine Herman Prince's canoe," the lady said.

"Herman Prince?" Danielle asked. "Hey, these are good."

"Yes, excellent," Donna said. "So who's Herman Prince?"

"It's one long story."

As she ate the sushi, Danielle looked at the woman. The healthy darkness of her face suggested someone who would live to be a hundred. Peeking out from under her long dress were two bunion-deformed feet, the toenails gray and splitting. Her hands looked arthritic and bony, the skin rough on the palms, and like stained parchment on the backs, blue veins between thin tendons. The woman now looked to her left, up the slope of her yard. "Come inna shade—I tell you. Unless you no like hea. But I tell you, is interesting."

The shade she referred to was a kind of half-circle gazebo out of sight of the overgrown back yard they had left. They sat on mildewed white plastic chairs arranged around a glass-topped table with a rusted frame. "It's pretty in here," Tricia said.

"Look, we don't have to take up your time," Danielle said.

"What?" Mollie Teruya said. "Is yoa time, not mines. Time all I get any more. I only like tell one story. You like hea?"

"Sure," Donna said, and then glanced at Danielle. The look said, let's just indulge the old lady, okay?

"'Kayden," Mollie Teruya said, "if you no mine. I nevah tol' dis story long time now, so I mus' tink 'kay?" She sat there for a few seconds, then cleared her throat. "Herman Prince was one beachboy Waikīkī long long ago, inna forties. A handsome paht-Hawaiian boy. 'Ass his canoe inna big shed. Anyways, every day, right out in front of da Moana Hotel and da Pink Lady he take touris' out and dey ride da waves every day. An' oh, so pretty Waikīkī back den—get lei stands, open spaces an' dakine—smaw town atmospheah. But anyways, was one family lived in rich rich rich paht Diamond Head, in one big house, named MacNeil, da faddah one business executive kine man, an' his wife one Chinese lady, Mei her name, one very nice lady. Dis house," and she pointed at the hedge behind them, "was dea dakine summah hideaway, so I know Mei way way back. So anyways, da MacNeils get

33

t'ree keeds, Donald, Robert, an' den Margaret, or Peggy. Peggy one very pretty girl, wit' dark hair and beautiful hapa featchas, you know, so pretty an' what? Elegant da right word, one serious girl, no mo' silly girl stuffs, good piano playah, good in skoo, dat kine. She shy too, an' very quiet. One day when she sixteen, she go beach wit' frien's, an' dey like take one canoe ride and go see Herman Prince. Well," and she sat back and raised her hands, then brought them down on her knees. "Was love at firs' sight yah? But Herman Prince only one beachboy 'kay? Make no mo' difference Peggy—she so in love wit' him dat she cannot tink shtraight ah? Dis Herman fall fo' her too, an' dream of marrying her and all li'dat. Was so in love dat couple ah? Herman one happy-go-lucky boy, love da ocean, love to gamble an' suck um up an' have fun. But he meet Peggy and like change his life, but he get no mo' notting but his canoe. He live in one cottage wit' odda beachboys, get no money. Meantime . . ." she stopped and thought here, while Danielle and Donna exchanged glances. Tricia seemed locked into listening, leaning forward with her chin on her fist.

"Meantime," Mollie Teruya said, "nobody inna MacNeil family know what is happening 'kay? Some days she gone all day, and what it was, on calm days when no big surf, da two of dem take da canoe an' dissapea aroun' pas' da Diamond Head Lighthouse. Nobody know whea dey wen' an' what dey did, but da family come suspicious, an' da braddahs go snoop an' fine out, see da canoe moveen along da beach an' outta sight wit' dose two figgahs in it, one dey know deah sistah, so da faddah fine out about Peggy an' how she get eyes fo' Herman Prince. He angry an' tell her no get interested in one beachboy—he get no money, he low class bum, he jus' one lazy loco boy wit' no fewtcha 'kay, he dis and dat. Plus, she only sixteen an' he what? Twenty? No, he no allow dis. Anyway, he so huhu about Herman Prince he want revenge fo' his even tinkeen dakine about his daughtah. Da braddahs too, dey very huhu about dis and try fo figgah ways to put one stop to dis. Dey know Herman Prince, dey know all his weaknesses.

Gambling is one big one 'kay? So da braddahs figgah dat if da canoe is da only ting keep Herman Prince happy, den dey figgah how fo' get da canoe, an' gambleen is how fo' do um. One cahd game. I know notting about dis, what game dey wen' play, pokah, whatevahs, but what happens is dey make nice wit' him an' invite him fo' one game, an' da guys, five, six of dem, dey drink an' slap backs and allkine happy stuffs li'dat yah? Herman Prince get dakined into one game. What? Lured I guess you say ah? Den da braddahs, dey cheat, and when da game a'mos' ovah, Herman Prince sees money onna table and probably tink, 'if I win den I impress Peggy's o' man', li'dat? So he bets da one ting he love mos' except fo' Peggy—his canoe, an' because da braddahs cheat, dey win an' take his canoe. Herman Prince miserable. Da braddahs happy, cause dey figgah finally how fo' stop dis ting wit' Peggy. Peggy meanwhile miserable too. But den in one big beef at her house she tells her faddah dat when she eighteen she decide what she do wit' her life. He say fine, whatevahs, but summahtime, you stay Moloka'i an' not Honolulu, so she end up what? Like one banished princess. She go back Honolulu to her las' year skoo, but da faddah an' braddahs watch her. She send messages t'rough frien's, tell Herman Prince will only be one year, den on'y six mont's. But Herman Prince not happy because of da canoe. Da family get afraid of him, tink maybe he come get his canoe, so what dey do? Dey put um on one barge an' ship um here, and dat canoe been in dat shed evah since."

She stopped, as if to get her breath, and seemed to have lapsed into thought.

"So what happened?" Tricia asked.

"Da res' of da story so sad," Mollie Teruya said. "Peggy, she squeeze fo' da days to go by. Da faddah watch her. But she confident dat she win out, if only Herman Prince wait fo her, an' her frien's say, he waiteen. On'y six mont's lef', come nineteen-fifty, an Herman go inna army, figgah he be one officer, maybe one general one day, den he can be wit' Peggy. He try fo' see her before he mus' go, an' cannot.

35

She miserable. Meantime," and there Mollie Teruya stopped again, and looked at them as if anticipating some skepticism. "I know," she said. "Long story, like I wen' tell you. Peggy's braddahs, dey get plenny money an' bored Waikīkī, go California. Den Peggy's faddah fall in love wit' one young touris' wahine, leave Mei, an' so Mei get dat house right dea. Da faddah keep da big one in Diamond Head. Pua Peggy and Mei come down Moloka'i like what I said, banished. Peggy turn eighteen, and figgah maybe Herman come down an' dey raise flowahs an' li'dat. 'Ass when da orchids get deah—Peggy, she put um onna canoe, an' I no remembah exackly, but was one plant, den laters anodda, den laters anodda yet. But Herman go Korea, an' end up missing in action, like dey say. He nevah come back. Peggy wait, wait, wait, an' Mei try fo' keep her spirits up, but by da time Peggy twenty-t'ree, den -foah, she see da writing onna wall 'kay? She hang herself. Right dea, in dat shed. Was in January, da fot', nineteen-fifty-five."

"Oh God," Danielle said.

"Mei live dea until lashear, den she die of ol' age. Pua Mei, we talk story every day, an' she so sad, have notting but her house and her plants. But she Chinese, so know how fo' enduah ah? She wattah da orchids onna canoe, make yahd pretty an' nice. An' dose plants, Mei keep um up, replaces ones dat die, an' da ones deah now been onna canoe maybe twenty years, more maybe, I fo'get."

Danielle looked at Donna, who had a distant, stricken expression on her face, and Tricia sat there, still with her chin on her fist, her eyes on Mollie Teruya. Then she took a small bite from her sushi and said, "But—" and did not continue.

"I know," Mollie Teruya said. "Is one very sad story."

Danielle looked at the box of sushi sitting on the table. "You guys want to take some of these?" she asked. Donna stared down at them as if she didn't know what they were, and Tricia continued to stare, not so much at Mollie as past her at some place in the distance.

"All right," Danielle said. "I'll save them for Kimo."

Danielle did not know why it was that the story, sad as it was, made her hate herself. Was it that the story made all the more glaring the stupidity and frivolity of her weaknesses? She didn't know. There was something about the idea of the ease with which she and Mark had split up that disgusted her. Well, I'll be around. Sure, we'll keep in touch. While she drove down the hill toward Kaunakakai to the Wines and Spirits store, she was aware that she held the steering wheel too tightly and drove too fast. For some reason, the story had aggravated something, like some hidden mental condition, so that her brain seemed to buzz with a strange anxiousness. Further, she did not see how she would be able to sleep another night in that room, which, she imagined, might have been Peggy MacNeil's room nearly a half a century ago. And that shed—the girl had strung herself up in that shed, and Danielle did not know if she could ever go in there again. Had she known about this, she would never have come down here, because there wasn't any chance now that anything would feel right to her.

She parked a half a block from the store and walked toward it, mingling with a group of four tourists, older ladies with cameras and men with sunburns. Just as she neared the door to the Wines and Spirits store, she made her way around the group past a man sitting on a plastic chair outside the store. He was dark, local, and looked up at her and said, "Where's the bus?" and then smiled. The tourists ignored him. Danielle stopped just as they did to take more pictures, and she flushed with a sudden, inexplicable anger at the man. She was about to tell him that she lived here, but his amiable smile put her off. And inside the store, she got her gin and stood at the counter, and found herself staring at a bottle tightly encircled at the neck with rope. She would have to go back to that house. When she paid for the gin, her hands shook.

But she would not be a wimp. She would take into consideration the simple fact that all this happened nearly a half a century ago. Probably all houses you see have a history that includes some tragedy or other. In that room someone died, in this room someone got raped, in that room over there someone committed suicide. Good stuff was the same—in this room people made love, that is, people who were really in love, not like herself and Mark but really in love, in that room maybe a baby grew up, in another someone painted a picture that hangs in some museum. It was only a house, and the way she would respond to the nonsensical superstition about whose room was whose and where someone strung herself up, would be to get a vacuum and some drape material and some cleansers and clean the house up, and then maybe get Kimo to help her unload the crap from that shed, the canoe included. Hell, canoes were worth a lot, and if it was still in good shape, then they could sell it.

When Kimo came home, his eyes red from his being in the water all day, she showed him the canoe. Standing in the weeds behind the shed, he stooped down and eyed the curved hull, and rose up and said, "It's fairly long, and whose did you say it was?"

"Herman Prince, a beachboy," she said. "Mollie Teruya, the lady next door, told us the story." She went on to tell the story, condensing it into a two-minute summary, and ended by saying, "She hung herself somewhere in here, maybe from one of those beams."

"Jesus," he said. "Give me the creeps. But hey," and he waved his hands toward the interior of the shed, "it happened so long ago. No mattahs. What you mean 'us'?"

"Tricia and Donna and me, but—" But what? She looked at the shellac peeling off the side of the hull. "What's the Hawaiian word for 'prince'?"

Kimo thought. "Ah, le's see—keiki ali'i I think. Is Tricia the little girl who never talks?"

"Yeah, that's her," she said. Then she said, "Keiki ali'i."

"Why you like know?"

"I don't know. I was just wondering."

"Might be warped," he said. "Get termites maybe too. But it's still worth big bucks."

"Maybe we can get it out and take a look at it."

"I can get some guys, couple days, we'll help."

"I'd just like to look at it."

"Hey, you like lef'ova lasagna?"

"'Lef'ova,'" she said. "I love that. Sure, steek um inna oven brah."

"Indeed," he said. "I will do just that, forthwith. And if you'd like, we have a tape of a Jackie Chan movie."

"Cool brah. Dakine intellectual stuffs do dakine to me."

Kimo snorted, gazed up at the sky, and went back through the weeds toward the house. She stood there looking at the side of the hull, then at the orchids. Well, Kimo was tired—the whole thing didn't seem to have impressed him that much. She looked around. All it would take would be a weed whacker and she could clear some space. But as far as she knew, there wasn't one around. So maybe she would get one. The will to start clearing a space then evaporated—it was too much trouble. She yawned and turned back toward the house where music drifted out of Kimo's bedroom window—Braddah John Ka'imikaua.

The presence of the music brought a little energy back to her, and she decided that if they didn't have a vacuum, she would find a broom and start cleaning. Kimo had claimed that he had cleaned everything—garans—but of course it was a bad job. It was getting dark, and the prospect of darkness produced a dull, nonsensical fear that she knew was because of that story. She snorted at the idea and got the broom and a dustpan and a plastic bag and stomped up the stairs to her room, and turned on the ceiling light and the standing lamp next to her bed. First, the grit under the bed, so that she wouldn't have to wake up to that squeaking when she pulled the bottle out. Just as she lifted one end of the cot to pull it aside, the roofing out back began to bong in the wind, with a regulated cadence that suggested someone lifting it and slamming it down rapidly. "Cute," she said, and pulled the bed around. The dust and grit underneath formed a bed-sized rectangle. The corrugated metal kept bonging, now in a random pattern. She sighed. The hell with it—she'd do it tomorrow.

She dragged the broom and dustpan to the corner and leaned them there, and just as she turned away she saw in the cone of light from the floor lamp something snagged in the broom—a hair. It was not hers because hers was light brown. She stooped down and pulled it out of the broom, and then went and sat on the bed and held it under the light. The hair was black, and as she ran it out, holding it between the thumbs and forefingers of her hands, it was two feet long. "Oh Jesus," she whispered. It was not an old woman's hair and it was not her own hair and no one had lived in this house except the old woman Mei for years, and so this had to be one of Peggy MacNeil's hairs, lying in the groove between two planks all these years. This had been her room. This was where she had waited for Herman Prince. She stooped down, still holding the hair, and reached under the bed for the gin bottle, and with the hair still entwined in the fingers of her left hand, she took a long gulp, swallowed, and waited for the burn to expand into her trunk. Breathing the hot vapor out, she looked at the hair, and then gently placed it on the nightstand.

She went downstairs to the phone and dialed Donna's number. She was there. "Can I come over for a while?" she asked.

"Okay," Donna said. She didn't sound enthusiastic about it. "I'll be here."

There was something about the tone of Donna's voice that scared Danielle a little. It was, she thought, Donna's Basket-Case mode, a relapse into that state of mind that made taking a bottle of pills possible, and she didn't know if it was a good idea for her to butt in. "You know, I can come tomorrow," she said.

"It's okay, come on over," Donna said.

Her cottage was just off the beach a few miles east of the Hotel Moloka'i, one house away from a shoreline arranged with rock-encircled fishponds. The cottage itself was a single large room with a kitchenette, living room area, and a bedroom and bath separated from those by hanging lau hala mats suspended from the beams of an open ceiling. But Danielle was not sure that she was there when she arrived and parked on the lawn because she could see no lights. She stepped hesitantly toward the door, and then stopped, her heart thumping a little at the idea that Donna could have done something since the phone call.

"I'm here," Donna called in a tired, dismissive voice.

"Hey," Danielle said, opening the door, "if it's not—"

"No no, come on in." She turned on a lamp. She was sitting on the couch with a Corona before her on the coffee table. "You want a beer? Or am I corrupting you?"

"No, it's okay," Danielle said, and went to the refrigerator. She got out a Corona and opened it, and went and sat in the chair across from Donna. "Beer is food."

"You know, when we paddle I can sometimes get a sniff of it in your breath."

"Well, it's sort of hard."

"What is it? Vodka?"

"Gin."

Donna looked at the dark windows, toward the ocean. She didn't say anything, and the look on her face wasn't right, as if something had happened that she didn't want to mention yet.

41

"Really," Danielle said, "if this is a bad time I can go."

"Have you ever been in love?" she asked.

"I don't know."

"I had about three or maybe four years of it. Maybe that's enough to last a lifetime and maybe it's not. I was probably too young to appreciate it. What I've got from that now is a son who doesn't call and this shack here. But—"

Danielle waited. Donna looked off toward the ocean again, long enough that Danielle found herself trying to invent something to say. Thinking of Mark again, she said, "Well, who knows what it is anyway?"

"You'd know it if it happened."

"I suppose you would. I mean, I have nothing to gauge it by. I thought it would be sort of dramatic when I left. It wasn't. It was cool with him. Everything was just so cool."

"My divorce almost killed me. Or I almost killed me because of my divorce. Judy told me that hers was a liberation. I asked her about that sense of failure, you know, that you blew your chance. She just said all she felt at getting out of it was success."

"Well, she's a little strange."

"I know. It was just one of those comparison things." Donna fiddled with magazines on the coffee table, then looked at Danielle, long enough that she began to feel a little embarrassed. "Your guy Mark wasn't love," she said. "Or you would have had some other sense of it."

"Well, Mark isn't someone I'd hang myself over. I guess that's the only way to put it."

Donna took a sip of her beer and put the bottle down. Then she put both hands on her face and rubbed slowly, and looked again at the dark windows. "And I tried to off myself over money," she said. "I feel like a stupid idiot. It's so fricking mortifying that it makes me want to—"

"'Fricking,'" Danielle said. She laughed. "My brother uses that word."

"It's a sanitized version of another word. Girls don't curse."

"Fucking A right they don't."

Donna snorted and shook her head. "I don't know," she said. "It's stupid and chickenhearted and—I don't know. I just got to thinking about it, that's all."

"I'm in her room," Danielle said. "That's probably why I'm here. I was going to clean the room and I found a long black hair. I'm in her room."

Donna's expression changed, into a kind of tense speculation. Then she said, "Maybe it's someone else's hair."

"No, it's hers," Danielle said. "So the story goes, she and her mother were the only people there, and her mother was older. And what else? She was twenty-four. I'm twenty-four. She was kind of exiled here. That's me."

"Don't get ideas."

"No, I mean in my case it's voluntary. I want to go back, but I'm not goin' back until I'm clean. I don't like the—what is that word?"

"Symmetry."

"Yeah, the symmetry of it. It scares me."

Donna looked at the windows again. After a silence she said, "And my biggest fear is money. Is that so god-damned cheap and embarrassing or what? Money. What a chicken."

"I think you're over that."

"I'm not sure," she said. "But I don't like myself much, I'll tell you that."

"Likewise." Then she added, "I mean I feel the same about myself."

"Do you ever wonder why life is so cheap?"

"Is it?"

"I don't know. Everybody fears death, and at the same time life is cheap."

Danielle felt a flash of heat run into her face. "You mean like my doing what I did even though I was warned about it?"

"Yeah. Or me with my pills. I mean what the hell was I thinking? I was drunk and miserable, so I took them. I woke up in a hospital with one doozer of a headache and a big question. Why did I do that? Money. So that's why I feel the way I do tonight. And maybe why you're here. Symmetry."

She thought about that. "Well, maybe you're right," she said.

"Okay," Donna said, and sat up and forward, her elbows on her knees. "We agree on something. So what else is new?"

"Nothing. It's just the hair. That's why I'm here."

Danielle was behind the shed arcing water at the orchids when Mollie Teruya appeared at the hedge, so she twisted the nozzle shut and went to the hedge. "I fine pitcha of yoa house," Mollie said. "You like see? Is from way way back, an' shows how pretty it was."

"Oh sure," Danielle said. "I'd like to see." She went down the hedge to the opening and around to Mollie. It was one of those old black and whites with squiggly edges. "You see onna steps is Peggy an' Mei," Mollie said.

Danielle squinted at the picture. True, the house was pretty, looked newly painted, with flowers around the foundation and healthy trees on the lawn. The two figures on the steps were difficult to make out, the one on the left Peggy, wearing a dress and white socks. Bobby socks, they were called, she thought.

"It was pretty," Danielle said. "It looks almost new."

"Dis tree one tangerine," Mollie said, pointing one bony finger at the picture, "an' dis one was avocado. Peggy sitting hea," and she pointed. "Oh, such a pretty girl she was."

Despite the somewhat murky detail, she could make out the hapa features and the long black hair, which made her pause a moment, her breath held. Peggy MacNeil sat up straight, with her hands in her lap, while Mei sat slightly hunched, her hands clasped under her chin. She was about to give the picture back to Mollie when she saw something else in the features: Peggy had an expression on her face, the stiff formality of a pose for a photograph mixed with a kind of haunted curiosity, her dark eyebrows raised as if she had asked a question and had been waiting for some time for an answer.

"When was this taken?" Danielle asked.

"Would be nineteen-fifty-one I tink. Was when dey get house painted ah? Take one pitcha. I remembah dat."

"You have a good memory."

"I let you keep um," Mollie said, "but I get only two pitchas of Mei, an' she was so nice."

"Oh that's all right," Danielle said. "Thanks, that's interesting."

In the evening Mark called. He was trying out a new cellphone. The sound of his voice immediately sent her heart up, so that she was aware of the thumping in her neck. "How'd you get my number?" she asked.

"Under 'Baker' in the Moloka'i phonebook," he said, and then after a pause, he said, "I miss you."

"I miss you too," she said, "but I've gotta straighten myself up a little. It takes work."

"Hey, I could help you with that. You know, there are therapies for this."

She knew what the tone of voice meant. Sex. And the attraction of the idea was such that she felt whatever resolve she had about her problem weakening. But she couldn't let herself get sucked into all that again. She was exiled. "You could come to Moloka'i," she said. "We could do all the homey stuff like hiking and appreciating the grandeur of nature and all that shit. I mean, we wouldn't have to get wasted every night to do that, right?"

"We didn't have to do that here," he said. "But sure, I could, but I can't right now."

"Business."

"Oh well," he said. "I guess you know the story there, right?"

Kimo came in, raised his eyebrows when he saw her on the phone. "Dad?" he whispered.

She shook her head, and he went to the refrigerator.

"Sorry," she said. "Kimo just came in."

"Yeah, well, I gotta sign off," Mark said.

"Okay."

"Take care," he said, and the phone went dead.

She sighed. What a horrible conversation, like one between strangers. But then, she thought, that's really what we were.

Kimo was reading the side of a box. More lasagna.

"Was him ah?" he said.

"Who?"

He snorted. "That guy Mark."

"Yeah, but it's not really your—"

"It is," he said, studying the box. Then he went and turned the oven on. "I know all about dat guy."

"From who?"

He snorted again.

"Dad wasn't supposed to mention this. This is not stuff that you have anything to do with."

"He's worried, 'ass all," Kimo said, and opened the box.

And she thought, that son of a bitch. "I can take care of myself," she said.

He pulled the foil dish of frozen lasagna out of the box. "Like shit you can," he said, and then looked thoughtfully at her. She looked back, studying those features that she supposed resembled hers somewhat, and didn't know what to say. "Vegetable lasagna again," he said. "You okay with that?"

"Yeah, I'm fine," she said.

She carefully wound the hair around a pencil until it formed a little shiny black ring, and then worked with a piece of thread until she managed to tie it in three places so that it held the form of a tiny circle. She put the circle of hair on the nightstand next to her bed. Then she tried to sleep, and the expectation of that piece of corrugated roofing slapping all night was almost reassuring, until she woke up at two or three to a strange, humid silence. There was absolutely no sound from anywhere, and she lay there in the bed, not moving, with the creeping sensation of something moving in the air around her. She was absolutely wide awake, lying very still, as if to see if whatever was moving might touch her. But it was no more than the child's fear of dark closets or ghosts, and she knew it. She sighed at the idea that she was buying into that, and sat up and turned the light on. The circle of hair was there. She got up and went to her suitcase and rummaged through it for the little purse she kept jewelry in, found a thin gold chain, and went back to the bed. There she picked up the loop of hair, and played the chain through it, and then put the chain around her neck and snapped the little clasp closed.

Then she turned the light off and lay on her back, the gold chain still a little cold on her skin. And then, indulging in this speculation against her better judgment, she pictured Peggy MacNeil, giving her own definition to the vague photograph. Danielle looked nothing like her—light brown hair while Peggy's was black, and Peggy looked as if she were much shorter, maybe even a little heavy. She couldn't even decide if Peggy had been pretty. But it didn't matter. She imagined her sitting on that long canoe, Herman Prince either behind her or ahead of her, it didn't matter, as they went through the water with Diamond Head looming above them on their left. And where did they go? Perhaps just past the lighthouse, where there was reef inside of the surfing waves, but then if it was low tide they could slide the canoe through channels to the little narrow beach there, the hill above covered with kiawe trees and long, parched grasses. Herman Prince, she imagined, would have nosed the canoe onto some break in the rocks that fringed the beach, and Peggy would have climbed over the seats to jump down into six or eight inches of water.

And then she saw Peggy MacNeil behind that shed watering orchids, not with a hose but with a heavy galvanized steel can, lifting it up to shoulder-level to pour it. There was grass then, not weeds, and Mrs. Teruya was much younger, maybe calling her to the hedge to pass cone sushi over. What she then imagined was that day when she was twenty-four, and walked out the back door of the house with a length of rope in her hand, looking at the beams in the shed and considering the logistics of getting up there to attach it to the beam so that she could hang herself. She did not cry. She had considered it, and decided. She looked around and saw the stepladder. She moved it to a spot on the dirt under a beam. Then she climbed it, her legs trembling because the ground she set it on was uneven, and the stepladder swayed. The rope in her hand was coarse, and when she got up high enough, she reached up and played one end over, and then knotted it, once. After this she worked at making a noose, not sure how to do it, and her hands trembled as she formed the circle and then worked the end of the rope into a slipknot. When she placed the rope around her neck, like some grotesque lei, the coarseness of the rope, its needle-ended fibers, hurt her neck on the sides and throat, but she continued, reaching behind her neck and pulling the slipknot down until it rested against the back of her neck, secured under the point of the back of her skull. Then she felt the cushioning on the back of her neck and pulled her hair out over the rope and let it fall behind her, and the rope's coarseness scraped the back of her neck. The stepladder swayed again, and she braced her knees against one of the steps.

Danielle sat upright and put the lamp on, her hands shaking so badly that she could barely turn the switch. Then she wrapped her arms around herself and whispered, "Oh God. Oh my God." It could have happened five hundred years ago. It didn't matter.

Donna called Danielle to tell her that the coach had called from Maui. The third canoe in their club would be manned by seven girls from Maui and four from Moloka'i, although plans could change—there were other girls on Maui who were about equal. It would be a Force-Five, Donna said, the one with the little chip in the thingie. The four would be The Airheads, Tricia Nakamoto as a reserve steersman, and Danielle as a reserve stroker. The other three would be left out. Donna wasn't worried about this—she paddled for distraction and exercise anyway, and she was sure that for the other two it wouldn't be a problem. In fact, Judy Beeman had seemed relieved to be left out, if that made any sense. Anyway, those that could would like to stop up at Danielle's place. The reason was just to say hello and to, well, they were interested in that story, which Tricia had repeated to them with enough detail that they wanted to take a look at the shed. Would that be all right? Sure, Danielle told her—just give me a chance to wash my face and eat a little breakfast.

The two SUVs arrived just as she finished her cereal. She had forgotten to take a gulp of gin, but felt good enough that she thought she'd try and skip it. As she had sat eating her breakfast, she had reached up, fifteen or twenty times, to touch the little circle of that single hair hanging on the chain. She still didn't know why she had done it, but because she had slept reasonably well after torturing herself with that image of Peggy MacNeil hanging herself, she woke up feeling not all that bad.

She met them out on the lawn, Donna and The Airheads, Marcia Soares and Tricia Nakamoto. She felt momentarily embarrassed about the two who weren't going, but the expressions on their faces seemed amiable enough that it made her feel okay. Tricia didn't want to talk, apparently, because she said "Hi," softly, and went past Danielle to the back, where the shed was. They watched her, then looked at one another. Donna held her shoulders up in a doubtful shrug.

"Anyway, I got juice," Danielle said. "Aloha Maid. Try come— you like I go get some?"

Marcia laughed. "Always so funny when haoles try talk pidgin."

"I practiceen," Danielle said.

"We already ate," Michelle Forten said. She was looking past the house toward the shed. "Tricia told us. It's so creepy. How can you sleep at night?"

"No problem," Danielle said. Just as she said that, the wind raised that section of corrugated roofing and it slapped several times before producing a watery, metallic rippling and then resting down. "See?" Danielle said. "This is what happens when I say it's no problem. Every time. Day, night." She stared up at the roof. "You'd think the damn thing would get it wrong once in a while."

They wandered past the house toward the shed, and she led them to the cleared space just inside the opening, and looked up. "One of these beams. Where's Tricia?"

Michelle Forten, Chrissy Moore, and Marcia Soares looked up at the ceiling beams, and Danielle went along the side of the shed to the back, followed by Donna. Back there they found Tricia, standing twenty feet away from the shed staring at the line of orchids. She didn't notice their presence—she seemed somehow mesmerized by what she saw.

"Yoo hoo," Danielle said.

She looked in their direction, and then walked toward them through the high grass, glancing again at the orchids. When she got up close to them, her eyes drifted down to the base of Danielle's neck. "What's that?" she asked.

"What? Oh, the chain." She shrugged. "Well, it's a little odd, I'll admit, but it's a black hair I found in my room—has to be one of Peggy MacNeil's hairs, since no one's been in that room except family."

Tricia squinted and moved very close, studying it. "I rolled it up and put thread on it," Danielle said. Just as she said that, she was sure that Tricia sniffed the air. She was momentarily taken aback. It appeared that she was sniffing for alcohol breath, and Danielle remembered that she hadn't had any. But then she might have been mistaken.

Tricia stood back, staring at the base of Danielle's neck until Danielle became a little tense. Why was she doing that? Then Tricia went back to where she had stood before, and turned and looked at the orchids. The roof began slapping and bonging again, this time lightly. Tricia looked up at it, then back toward Danielle and Donna, then back at the orchids.

"What's with her?" Danielle asked Donna. "Doesn't it bother you the way she looks at you sometimes?"

Donna shrugged. "She always was a little what? Mysterious?" She turned around to look back toward the house. "Oops, what's this? An invasion?"

Kimo came along the side of the shed followed by two locals, both of them stocky and dark. "Eh," Kimo said, "dis Daryl and Hayward Kama. Come fo' look at da canoe."

They stopped by the side of the shed, and behind them a single-file line of The Airheads and Marcia Soares made their way around them, stomping down more of the tall grass. "So how Auntie Bea?" Marcia asked.

"She's fine," Daryl Kama said. "Get really healthy now, no mo' dakines because they fixed her blood sugar an' stuff. She even swims too ah?"

"Well, like I say, tell her I send my alohas 'kay?"

"Yah, we tell 'er."

"We come cause no mo surf," Kimo said. "Laters maybe."

"You guys want juice?" Danielle asked.

"Nah nah," Daryl said.

"No, you do," she said. She went back toward the house. What? Get a couple of six packs of it and whatever bags of chips they had. She found a jar of olives in the refrigerator, two half empty bags of tortilla chips on the counter, and put them in a plastic bag, and then picked up two six-packs of Aloha Maid from the floor and, the bag handle around her wrist and the six-packs one on top of the other in her hands, made her way back outside to where everyone was now gathered behind the shed.

Tricia was talking to Kimo while the Kama brothers were talking with The Airheads. Apparently Tricia wanted Kimo to hand her the orchids, one by one, so that she could rest them in the partial shade over by Mrs. Teruya's hedge. Danielle rested the juice and chips and olives on an overturned fifty-five gallon drum by the corner of the shed. One by one, the flowers came down, pulled away from the canoe so that their gray roots tore off and remained glued to the wood. Tricia carried each one to the hedge. The Airheads were still with the Kama boys, talking with a peculiar earnestness, and Danielle imagined what they might be saying: like surfing is so majorly cool, and whoa, we'd like to try it out too. What about us flying over to Lahaina later, like we can cruise Front Street and maybe party a little. I mean like if you guys can spare the time. I mean like, omigod, Front Street is so awesomely cool, and we know all the places where we can like kick back, have a brew or two and just hang.

No, their expressions didn't seem to lend themselves to that kind of conversation. The Kama brothers were doing most of the talking, and the Airheads stood there looking up at them, their bearing peculiarly deferential.

When the orchids were off the canoe and resting in the dappled sunlight along the hedge, set by Tricia precisely the same distance apart as they had sat on the canoe, the Kama brothers went over to Kimo, and they studied the canoe.

"'Kay," Kimo called, "here's how we can do it. Daryl an' Hayward get under the middle 'kay? You guys get ends, I get whatevahs. We lif' um slow an' set um down easy cause dis one ol' canoe 'kay?"

Danielle and Donna went to the end closest to the path alongside the shed, and The Airheads went to the end closest to the hedge. Tricia went just behind The Airheads. They moved themselves through the weeds and to the canoe, which rested on three sawhorses with rug cushions where the hull met the wood, the sawhorses themselves set up on a low bench. Kimo got between the Kama brothers, and when he said, 'okay', they lifted slowly, and the canoe went up. They walked sideways, very slowly, until they were out in the weeds, and lowered the canoe to the ground, the weeds keeping it upright on its rounded hull.

"'Kay," Kimo said.

"What about the whatchucalls?" Danielle asked.

"Gotta be in the shed," Kimo said. "I bet they took um off for shipping—less chance for damage?"

The canoe looked long enough. It had all six seats, and the stabilizers under the seats looked hand-hewn. "Wae," Hayward Kama said. "Maybe even ʻōhiʻa root. ʼAss what da olʼ Hawaiians used. It means ʻspreaderʼ. Is so da canoe no fold in." Kimo was back in the shed, peering into the junk leaning against the walls. "Hui," he called, and the Kama brothers turned. Kimo leaned a long section of wood out, that looked like a filled-in wishbone. It was a bow-cover, complete with what Donna called the ʻthingieʼ, which was the manu, or upward projection, the elliptical point that gave the canoe its classic shape. Hayward Kama carried the piece out to the canoe, and placed it on one end. "Nope," he said. "Oddasai," and he carried it to the other end and placed it there. "See this?" he said to Chrissy Moore, and she looked. "Screw holes heah," and he pointed. "Dis like one Malia design, but like a little tubby da canoe ah?"

"Tubby?" she said.

"Yah," he said. "Da whatchucall—beam, is wide." The other end piece came out, and Kimo fitted it in place and stood back.

"We need ʻiakos and ama."

"Got um," Daryl called. He carried out the banana-shaped ama, or float, made of some lighter-colored wood, and then went back in and came out with the two booms, whose ends suggested a straight line, but whose middles were looped slightly. "Dis made of hau," he said. "Is old, dis canoe. Dat float is wiliwili." Kimo went and got a bag of chips and a six-pack of Aloha Maid, and he and the Kama brothers opened the chips and three cans, and ate and drank, their eyes on the canoe.

Danielle walked around it, high-stepping in the weeds. The wood was of different hues, because parts had replaced other parts, although most of the canoe appeared to be made of a single log. She reached out and touched the hull, realizing as she did so that she was holding her breath. Tricia materialized beside her, staring at it. On the other side of the canoe Donna stood, staring down at it, then up at Danielle and Tricia. Danielle reached up and touched the little loop of hair hanging on the chain.

"You know," she said, "I've been sort of half-thinking."

Donna snorted softly and looked at her, a strange expression on her face, a sort of calculating speculation, as if she were visualizing something. "Me too," she said. "And I haven't been sleeping that well lately. It's obvious."

"It is," Tricia said. "Isn't it?"

"So that makes three of us," Danielle said.

"Then it's three of us," Donna said.

"Nope. We need a crew."

"What about the coach?" Tricia asked. "We tell him the deal's off, right? It's only fair that we tell him."

"Right," Danielle said. "But we need a crew."

"Co-ed," Donna said.

"Nope, this is the Na Wahine O Ke Kai. Keyword, wahine."

"What about just taking it across?" Donna asked. "Isn't the channel race somewhat of a stretch?"

"Well," Danielle said, "it's true, we can—"

"No," Tricia said. She stared at the canoe, thinking. Then she looked at them with a strange aggression on her face, an expression unlike her. "We get one chance for this," she said, "and it has to be done right. We're taking Herman Prince's canoe home in style."

They both looked at her. That she had put it so succinctly and so out in the open surprised Danielle. Tricia had been way ahead of them.

"It's complicated," Danielle said. "There are rules. You have to have ten."

"Look," Tricia said, "I don't care about that. Put old ladies in it. I don't care about the race and I don't care if it takes twelve hours.

I'd give my right arm to do this. Of course that wouldn't make sense because I couldn't paddle, but I'd give anything to do this. I don't even care why—but I know why and you know why and it's almost cheesy. You want cheese? Then it's for the glory of love," and at that they all laughed, her little truncated giggle buried in the volume of theirs.

"Let's not sing, okay?" Donna said. "Oh God, let's not sing."

After a few seconds of silence, Tricia said, "This is a really strange coincidence, you know. Just the idea that we paddle, and the canoe would be here, that the channel race would be just ahead of us."

"Well," Danielle said, "there are canoes around. This is Hawai'i."

But Tricia seemed almost not to be listening. "It is strange," she said, "how it would be here. It's a strange coincidence."

Danielle and Donna exchanged glances, and then Donna came out with a subtle shrug. Well, that's Tricia, she seemed to be saying.

Danielle looked around. The Airheads were talking with the Kama brothers. She made eye contact with Chrissy Moore and jerked her head. Chrissy came through the weeds to the canoe. "What?" she asked.

"What about us taking this across?"

"You mean the race?"

"Yeah."

"Uh-uh," she said. "That's crazy." Then she apparently saw Danielle's expression, and said, "Look, we worked our asses off for this. I mean, the plan was the plan right? I don't see how we could even, like, qualify this thing. I mean look at it. We don't even know how much it weighs. It's supposed to be four hundred pounds or more. How do we know it won't fall apart?" She looked away from them, as if aware that she was blowing them off.

"It was just an idea," Danielle said.

Chrissy seemed now to be thinking it over. "I mean, every cent I make goes into getting into this race," she said, this time more an apology than a declaration.

"I know," Danielle said. "We wouldn't be thinking of doing well or anything, just taking it across. Besides, you guys made the crew."

The last statement made her shake her head, and then she shrugged. "Sorry," she said. "I have to stick with this."

She went back to Michelle and the Kama brothers.

"I guess I'd go too if I was a sure thing," Danielle said. "Besides, she probably sees having to spend more money if we take this one."

"Okay, so it's three," Donna said. "Seven to go."

Marcia Soares, who had been standing inside the remains of the shed with Kimo, came over to them. While Danielle explained their idea, she looked at the canoe. When Danielle was finished, she said, "'Kay, you can pencil me in. I gotta wedge my 'okole in da Force-Five, but no mo' wedge 'okole in dis buggah. Ho, fat da canoe."

"Four," Donna said. "That makes four of us."

"Eh Kimo!" Marcia called, "you like put two grapefruits in yoa tee shirt an' come wit' us?"

Kimo came over, the nearly empty chip bag in one hand, grease shining on the other, and said, "Hah?"

"We taking dis across," Marcia said. "Da race I mean. Ho, pig, lemme have." She pulled a handful of chips out.

Kimo looked at the canoe. "Why?"

"Because," Danielle said.

"What you do with it when you get there?"

"I don't know."

"What about the club? Won't the coach be pissed?"

"Maybe, but we're just reserves. They don't need us. I think they just sort of tolerate us—you know, h'm, we gotta include the Moloka'i girls."

Kimo thumped the hull with his knuckles, pulled on a seat, leaving oval fingerprint marks that showed a rich red-brown. "No cracks," he said. "But it's shaped funny kine—is like one Malia but then not like one Malia. Like the hull is heavier? Good for open ocean I guess. But you gotta do allkine stuffs to get um ready. I mean paperwork an' money and li'dat."

"Three hundred fifty dollars," Donna said. "Let's see, we need to sign waivers like always, we need gender verification and proof of age. Gender verification is no problem though—someone shows up with boobs and a five o'clock shadow, then they ask for proof. And as far as I can remember, you can register up to and including the morning of the race. Then there's like form eight hundred or something like that. It's gotta be weighed and measured and so on."

"Kimo," Marcia said, "you like verify my gendah?"

"Laters," he said. "'Kay, an' what about da escort boat? 'Ass gotta qualify too you know." He looked again at the canoe, backed up, walked around it, then waved the chip bag around. "I talk to Hayward about what kine shellac or whatevahs you put on um."

They all looked at the canoe. Who would provide an escort boat? They'd have to pay someone who would be willing to stay with them if it took them until midnight to get the canoe across.

"We'll look into that," Danielle said.

"An' you need a trailer," Kimo said. He shrugged, looked down at the canoe, and then walked off.

"It won't work," Danielle said.

"It will too," Tricia said. "We'll make it work."

"I'll call Judy Beeman," Donna said. "Let's see. We can ask around if there are any paddlers without canoes. There's gotta be some."

"Yeah, rejects like us," Danielle said.

"It'll work," Tricia said. "I'm gonna go buy some tarps to put over this."

"I gotta go too," Donna said.

By the time they had all left, Danielle had receded back into serious doubt about the whole ridiculous enterprise. Ten year olds came up with grand plans too. And ten year olds were capable of seeing the impracticality of their plans. This enterprise, conceived by adults, was impractical. It was not that they couldn't do it, at least technically. The problem was that she was frightened of the idea of getting into a canoe for a forty-one mile open ocean race with people who weren't that good even at quarter-mile regatta sprints. What she had wanted was to be in a canoe with seasoned paddlers. This crew would only embarrass themselves, half of them puking their guts out. They would huli the canoe fifty times, have it wash away in a wave, crash it into other canoes.

Then she thought that the decision to take that canoe across unnerved her enough that the prospect of sleeping alone in the house became a more tangible concern. It was that she had acknowledged Peggy MacNeil and Herman Prince. That was it. Now that they were acknowledged, the images of those dead people in her mind became somehow threatening, as if everyone's looking at his canoe and thinking of Peggy MacNeil had slowly but inevitably awakened these ghosts that had been sleeping for fifty years. Kimo would be gone soon, at least during the weekdays, and she wasn't sure if she could handle the empty house, especially at night.

This fear was corroborated again: even though Kimo was in the other room, she found herself awake at three in the morning, listening to the occasional bonging of the corrugated roofing, and then listening to the silence itself, which hung so heavy in the air that she became convinced that there was a presence nearby, either Mei or Peggy or even Herman Prince himself. She even thought she heard some kind of whispering, some soft, plaintive voice talking to her, but reasoned that the rustle of the leaves outside sounded a little like whispering. She got up and sat on the edge of the bed, then reached under to get the bottle. One good swig ought to do it. She did that, recapped the bottle and put it away, squeaking it over the grit, and then waited to drift off to sleep. But she did not drift off—she began, again, imagining those trips Peggy and Herman Prince took from Waikīkī around the Diamond Head lighthouse and to some secluded little beach out there along the steep kiawe and grass covered bluffs that ran down to the thin beach and the water. And she began to imagine conversations between the sixteen year old and the beach-boy, because it was so long ago, conversations characterized by more formality than would be used today: and how are your parents? My parents are fine. Is that flower in your hair from a tree in your yard? Yes, and we have pua kenikeni trees, and ginger in all the corners, and this is an orchid. My mother grows the most beautiful orchids. Where would they be sitting? The canoe would be up on the beach, and perhaps they would sit each in a seat, facing one another, their knees respectfully separated by two feet or so. She would look at his forearms on his knees, roped with veins and dark from his being in the sun all day, and her heart would begin to beat hard enough that she would fear his seeing it in her neck. The desire for him, so pure and innocent in its elemental force, would make her wish the sun was already down, so they could—

She could not exhaust herself into sleep with these speculations, and got up at five in the morning. She ate a banana, and waited for the dawn, and when it became light enough for her to see, she went outside and along the side of the shed, the now trampled grass making a lane that went right to the tarp-covered canoe. She pulled the tarp out from under some bricks and pulled it back to reveal the first two seats. The canoe was still not lashed with its outrigger boom, so she could not sit in it because it would tip over, but she placed the flat of her hand on one of the seats, on the koa that still had a patina of dust and grime on it, and knew that Peggy MacNeil had once sat in this seat, as she had probably sat in all the other seats. Herman Prince, too, had sat in every seat. Although it frightened her to think of going out with novices, actually frightened her to think of going out at all, she realized that she would do this or die trying, because underneath any explanation or motivation provided by Tricia or anyone else, she wanted one thing: to rescue something from Mollie Teruya's story that could be thought of as just, or right. What it had to do with her, if anything, she wasn't sure, but there was a weird hint there somewhere, one she couldn't identify.

She noticed that the Kama brothers had braced the canoe with pieces of wood, so that it would not tip over. She looked around, at Mollie Teruya's hedge, then at the back of the old shed, seeing the higher beams through the open back part. She braced herself by gripping the rails on each side of the canoe, and tested its stability. It would not fall over, so she lifted her left leg over the rail and got in. She sat down slowly, holding the rails. So. Peggy MacNeil had sat here. Her childhood coach had told all of his young paddlers that canoes had souls, had minds and memories, and now she was sitting in a canoe that had beautiful, and then horrible memories. The wind picked up a little, and she waited for the sound of metal flapping on the roof, but no sound came, and the fact that no sound came made her wary, and then afraid, and then it was as if the canoe were buzzing slightly, as if it, too, had been awakened like the ghosts of the two lovers, and she realized that she had been sitting there holding her breath, and had to think to breathe, and after she had taken three deep breaths, she looked down at her feet planted on the old wood, and whispered, "Oh God, it's awful. It's awful."

As for what she had thought of as a ridiculous enterprise, she now thought that once they had acknowledged the ghosts, and the canoe, they had in effect made a promise, and now they had to keep it.

Kimo was in the kitchen eating cereal when she got back. "Whatchu doeen?" he asked.

"I wen' check da canoe," she said, and waited to see if he would pick up on the game.

"And how did you find the canoe?"

"Is dakine, raddy fo' da race except fo' shellac but. An' fricken fawm eight whatevahs. Oddawise, garans."

"I'm delighted to hear that it is," Kimo said, carefully pronouncing each word.

"I so fricken delighted I cannot stand um. Ho, get anxious li'dat."

"Today I have decided to ride waves on my board," he said. "Recall that I have but a few more days before I depart. Will you be all right here, alone?"

"Yah. I figga, chance um. No mo nobody fo talk wit', but hey, can do um."

"That was more than competent," he said. "There's still something absent in what we refer to as 'the lilt', and the haolified accent just doesn't catch the rhythms and cadences of pidgin, which are 'felt' rather than intellectualized, if you know what I mean, but you progress well. B plus."

"F'real? Ho, tanks ah?"

"Keep up with it, and we shall converse laters. Check that, later."

"'Kayden. Listen, where are we gonna get an escort boat?"

"Lemme ask aroun' 'kay? Plus, can ask coach too, right? Or will he be so pissed that he'll make sure you don't get one?"

"I don't know. Donna's gonna call him and tell him we're out of it. I don't know. There's plenty of time though. I'll keep asking."

Kimo was gone within five minutes, passing Tricia Nakamoto on his way out. Danielle peered through the living room window at them talking briefly, and then Tricia came up the walk to the front door. Why now? She had already thought that there was something about Tricia that had become more than merely annoying to her, and now, opening the door, she felt the same annoyance wash over her, even though Tricia might ordinarily be welcome as a means of passing the time.

"I have a question," Tricia said.

"Shoot."

"The hair," and she pointed at Danielle's neck. "Would you think there'd be more?"

"Maybe, I don't know."

"Would you mind if I looked?"

"Uh, no, I guess not." Tricia came in, and looked around with a wary curiosity. Danielle pointed to the stairs, and Tricia followed her up. Just before entering the room, Danielle remembered the gin bottle under the bed, and felt her face flush. And when her face flushed she became angry. She wanted to turn and ask Tricia flat out why she was being so nosy, but did not.

Inside the room, Tricia immediately looked down at the floor, and then stooped down to look in the cracks between the boards, then got down on her knees so that her eyes were within five inches of the crack. "Wait," Danielle said, "here's a pencil." Tricia took the pencil and put the point into one of the larger cracks, and dug grit out, then a toothpick, then what looked like a bobby pin. She ran the pencil point along the crack, and then stopped.

"Here's one," she whispered. She pulled carefully at the hair, which, as it came up out of the crack, brought dust and grit with it. Once it was out, she carefully ran her fingers along the hair, pulling it out until she came to the end. Two feet at least. "'Kay," she said, and stood up. She took a little plastic baggie out of her shorts pocket, and carefully put the hair in, and again got down on her knees with the pencil. Danielle was about to ask what she was up to, but decided not to.

Tricia found eleven hairs. She never got to look under the bed, where the bottle was.

"They're all black," she whispered.

"What's the idea?"

"I'm making some loops, just like that one. For any of us who go." She stared at it a moment, and then said, "You know, I imagine it."

"What?"

"The suicide. I keep trying to imagine it. That she actually did that, tied a knot in a rope and then looked at the beams, and picked one." She looked around the room, and then settled her eyes on the closet, with the line of Danielle's clothes hanging there. "Your clothes," she said.

"Well, I guess it's natural to imagine it," Danielle said. "I guess I imagine it too. And yeah, that's my clothes."

"Those are your clothes from Honolulu?"

She stared at Tricia. "That's my clothes from Honolulu."

Tricia stared at them, thinking.

"Doesn't it scare you a little?" Danielle asked. "I mean us and the canoe and the ocean?"

Tricia looked out the window toward Mrs. Teruya's house. "It terrifies me," she said. "But then, almost everything does."

"Really?"

"It's just me," she said. "All my life. A while ago I just had to accept the idea that I'm one of those people who can't do certain things. I mean, being at the University taught me that. I—"

When she didn't continue, Danielle said, "What?"

"I don't know. I always wished I had guts." She looked back at Danielle's clothes. "But I don't. So I have to figure out how to have guts. It's like I have to cross the line."

"Okay," Danielle said. "We all have to do that I guess."

When Tricia left, Danielle went back upstairs to her room, and stood before the closet. So these were her Honolulu clothes. What else would they be? She saw the line of little, sexy dresses she had worn when she went out with Mark. One of them, and she pulled a light blue one aside, shuddering when the hanger hook scraped on the old pipe it hung from, had a wine stain on it. She looked at the faint stain—it was at a party for a friend, down at Restaurant Row, where she had spilled the wine. As a matter of fact it had been a wild night, one of those nights which she barely remembered the next morning, which was a little before the evening she failed to remember at all. Then she wondered why she'd brought all this to Moloka'i. She could have stored it at her father's place.

When they got to practice that evening, The Airheads were not there. "So," Donna said. "They blew us off."

"Well," Danielle said, "for them, like racing in like a Force-Five with their bangles and toenail polish and makeup is like so awesomely cool and can you like imagine what it'll be like when they like, come in at the Hilton Hawaiian Village? I'm all like, wow and double wow."

There were four of them: Danielle and Tricia in one two-man, Marcia and Donna each in one-mans. There still had been no word from The Barf Queen. By the time they got back an hour and a half later, they were exhausted, and making their way to shore, they saw

The Airheads on the beach, both of them sitting in the grass under a tree. "So what's with this?" Donna called. "Slumming?"

It was not slumming. They were both so tired that they could barely stand. They had spent the day helping the Kama brothers and some other locals, even high school students, restore an old fishpond, carrying rocks as big as basketballs and like, thrashing their feet and knees. They had no makeup on, and their hair was a mess. The expressions on their faces were an unfamiliar blend of inward-turning thoughtfulness and exhaustion. They just didn't look like The Airheads.

"So you wanna go out on a short one?" Danielle asked.

"We were like talking with Daryl and Hayward," Michelle Forten said, "and I'm like, hey you wanna come to the beach when we leave in the race? And he's like, okay and all? So I'm all, okay, so here's the info, but he's like, are you taking the koa? I'm like, nah, we're taking a Force-Five, and he's all, that's too bad, because I think one of the best things you can ever do is take koa across the channel. Koa is spiritual, is the wood of the old war canoes. Like a Force-Five is made out of guess what? Du-uh. I mean, can you say 'fiberglass'? I'm like wow, he's right—"

"So we're ditching the club, I mean for now," Chrissy Moore said. "I guess it was just the way he explained it. I'm all, Jesus, he's right. He said that koa has like a life to it. I mean I got this really like wow I didn't know that feeling?" She paused and looked at her hands. "Maybe—"

"Look," Danielle said, "if it's a problem with the money, there are enough of us that we can absorb it."

"Well—"

"Everything gets divided by seven or eight or something like that."

"Well, if it's okay with you," Chrissy said.

"It's okay," Donna said.

"So I guess we're kind of sold on this," Michelle said. "We should take koa across the channel. We'll worry about the other next year."

"So it's six," Donna said.

"And they said it's gotta be blessed, and have a name," Michelle said.

"Blessing I can get," Marcia said. "Easy. Or maybe da Kama boys know somebody."

"And the name is *Keikialiʻi*," Danielle said.

Kimo apparently wanted to hang out with friends in the evenings as much as possible before he left, so when Danielle found herself alone at the house in the evening, she decided to go have drinks at the Hotel Molokaʻi, which she hadn't tried yet, and called Donna to see if she would like to join her. No answer. So she went alone. Donna wasn't a great fan of it anyway, had told her once that on Friday nights they had music outside on the little, covered lanai, and it was usually crowded, but mostly with older haoles and tourists who tended to get smashed as the evening wore on. The better the music, she said, the drunker the tourists. Danielle would have stayed home and done her drinking there, but for a little rush of rebellion she felt at Kimo's presumptuous tendency to act like an older brother when he wasn't.

But the idea of going there soured as she drove the Tercel down to Kaunakakai and turned left to go to the hotel—she was a little looped already, and feared being stopped by a cop who would ask her to tiptoe along a curb. And when she got to the hotel and walked across the dirt and grass parking area to the lanai, she found that it was so crowded that she ended up wedged in a corner at a little table, watching a Hawaiian group singing and strumming their instruments while the tourists sang along. Songs she liked: "Pua Lililehua," "Sweet

Lei Mokihana," and some Braddah Iz songs. Because she was a little looped, sound itself seemed softened and made a little flat and tinny and distant, and she ordered a gin and tonic. And then she more or less lost her sense of time, existing way inside her loopiness and watching, and someone who introduced himself as Gary Osborne was talking to her while she nodded and answered his questions: are you from here? Yes. Have you been to the east end? Yes. And then the waitress banged into their table and sloshed her drink a little, and she steadied it and looked all the way across the crowd and saw young people sitting on benches and chatting just outside the lanai, and wished she had friends with her. A dish of pupus appeared on their table. Teri beef pieces on little sticks. She picked one up and ate it, poked her tongue a little with the stick.

"Because I just bought a place out there," he told her, his voice raised because of the music. Who was he? She stared at him, took a sip of her drink.

"Oh that's nice," she said. Ozzie something? Or Gary?

"So what do you think? Like to?"

"Like to what?" she asked.

"My question from before," he said. Was he handsome? She squinted. Yes, he was. Curly hair, mid-thirties, well tanned, one of those people who took fitness seriously. And then she thought, maybe too seriously, because he seemed somewhat bulked up wearing his golf shirt with a logo she couldn't read. He was a little too tan for a guy with blonde hair.

"Could you repeat your question?"

"I asked you if you'd like to come out tomorrow and see the place? It's an old house but has no termite damage, and the water is so blue you wouldn't believe it. I'm going to keep it as a weekend place."

"Oh that's nice," she said. She looked out over the sea of aloha-wear clad bodies, and tried to remember being asked that question. "Did you say you weren't from here?" she asked.

"California?" he said.

"Oh of course," she said. "You told me that, didn't you?"

"Yes," he said, and then he seemed to stare at her too long. "And I'm staying right here. I told you that too, I think."

"Yes, you did."

So what was the plan? Was she supposed to go with him to his east end house now? No, tomorrow, she thought he had said. In the meantime, what? Was she supposed to be invited to his room now? And if she was, what was she supposed to do then? Was she supposed to say yes? Was this supposed to end in his bed with giggles and hushed, conspiratorial whispering about the condom? She considered this, and thought that it might be simply destined to happen, and that Ozzie or whatever knew all the proper protocols for this negotiation and it would simply happen because he was earnest and on his game and she was tired and drunk and guessed that this was why she came here in the first place and it would happen and then she would leave in the morning. That was cool. Nice knowin' you. Call any time. Like let's keep in touch.

"This would make the third of these places I've bought," he said.

"The third? Oh my."

"I like property," he said. "What is it your state has as a motto? The life of the land is perpetuated in real estate?" And he laughed, shook his head and held his hands up. "I take it back," he said. "Sorry."

"It's righteousness," she said. "I think." She was tired. It was almost as if she should just go to sleep right at the table, or go with him.

"I know," he said. He looked around. "Can I get you anything? Another drink?" And then his skin seemed unnaturally tanned.

"Did you go to a tanning salon?" she asked.

"What?" He hadn't heard her.

She looked out over the crowd. Outside, on the bench, she saw two girls sitting there, both with dark hair and hapa features. Well, what now? She reached up and held the loop hanging on her chain between her thumb and index finger, felt the tiny knots and the curved strands of hair sliding over other strands of hair, and began to feel uneasy. And then she was scared.

"Oops," she said. "I see my friend over there."

"Friend?" he said, looking around. "Listen, let me get you another drink."

The two girls got up and went away. The bench was empty. "My friend Peggy," she said. "She just showed up. I mean I think she did." She got up from her chair. "It was nice to meet you," she said. "But I have to go. She's waiting."

"I don't see anybody there," he said. "C'mon, let me get you another drink." He stood up. "And my offer's still open."

"Oh, thanks," she said. "But—you see, my friend. She's waiting." She moved away from the table, rocky on her feet, and made her way out to the parking lot. There, trying to remember where she had parked the car, she looked back. He had not followed her. Away from the noise, and hearing the water slosh against the rocks, she felt her mind coming back to her. She had had to lie her way out of that one, and now she had to negotiate the car back home. She took a series of deep breaths. She'd done it before, she could do it again.

During the next three days, Danielle, Donna, and Tricia sanded the hull, most of the work on the side that had faced the sun all those years, and sanded the inside and the ama and 'iakos. The restoration also included buying new screws for the front and back tops and for the seats, and wood filler for little fissures and erosions in the koa. Each late-afternoon gathering made for a little party, sometimes joined by Mollie Teruya with her sushis and lef'ova chicken and all li'dat. Danielle did think of these gatherings as parties, and so went upstairs to take sips of gin while the other two sat around taking rests drinking Coronas and eating chips and lef'ovas. Chrissy Moore and Michelle Forten showed up late on the third day, after much of the work was done. While they were sanding in the fading light, Danielle looked at Chrissy and said, "Piling up the overtime, huh?"

"No, actually we like cut some of our hours, you know, because of the stuff we're doing. Do you sand the underside of the seats too?"

"No, they're okay. Stuff?"

"You know, fishponds and like that. It's like a disaster for my savings book."

"Doesn't that compromise your Toyota dream?"

Michelle, who was listening in, rose up from the hull and laughed. "On hold," she said.

"Yeah," Chrissy said, "and get this. Daryl and Hayward have like four younger brothers and sisters. We were over there and it's like a madhouse. Uh, do you hear a strange bell ring?"

"Uh-oh," Michelle said. "Water seeking its own level."

"So you kind of like them, huh?" Danielle asked.

"Oh, they're just nice guys," Chrissy said. "Nothing like serious there, I mean nothing yet."

"Kinda sorta," Michelle said. "You know, like somewhere between a remote possibility and a faint probability?"

"Ah," Danielle said, patting the dust off her piece of sandpaper. "That I understand."

By the time they had finished with the sanding, so that the outside of the hull seemed smooth wherever you touched it, arrangements had been made with Hayward to bring up the right shellac to put on it, and he did show up with two gallon cans that had no labels on them—my uncle's shellac 'ass why, is ol' but still slosh inside ah? Is fo' boats. Plus my uncle use um to touch up stuff aroun' da house too ah?—and they dipped their brushes into the amber liquid and swept the shellac along the hull, instantaneously transforming the wood into the rich, reddish-golden hue worthy of the best gift-shop koa. Looking at the finished canoe, thinking, this is the *Keikiali'i*, Danielle became convinced that the canoe was up to the challenge. Whether or not she was up to it was another matter.

"Well," Donna said, "there he is."

"He?" Tricia said. "Oh yeah, prince."

"So pretty da canoe," Mollie Teruya said. "Look like da day it come up hea."

They stared at it in silence.

"One more coat and we're done," Donna said. "Herman says it has to have two coats. Oh, I mean Hayward. But we'll come tomorrow. You can come too Tricia?"

But Tricia wasn't listening. She stared at the canoe, her mouth slightly open, and after a silence jerked her head back toward Donna. "What?" she said. "Did you say something?"

She walked in the house, a small bag containing another bottle of gin under her arm, and heard Kimo on the phone: "—but you no need call here any more 'kay? She needs time off 'kay? You do whatevah you do 'kay? But leave her out of it."

Silence. Who else could it have been but Mark? Danielle tiptoed to the stairs and went up to hide the bottle under the bed, and when she got back down the stairs she heard Kimo talking: "—don't know you, brah, but put it this way: bein' wit you made her sick 'kay? So jus' lay off." And after another silence: "Yah yah yah, I know, none of my business ah? I jus' telling you. Yah yah. No problem. Bye."

She went into the kitchen. "You could have simply taken a message you know."

"I didn't know you were here."

"It's all very noble of you to try to protect me, but look, I can take care of myself, and he's not a monster or a stalker or whatever."

"I not so sure of that, sista," Kimo said, folding his arms across his chest. "Look where he put you."

"I'm all right, really," she said.

"No you're not. You think I cannot smell um? Shit, you get da blinders on big time ah?"

"So I subsist a little on it, so what?"

"'Kay, whatever. It's your liver, not mine."

"Stay outta my business."

"'Kay, whatever."

"I'm serious. Besides, I'm older than you—just lay off, like you told him, okay?"

"Shit," he said, "you one adolescent."

"Don't get smart with me," she said, a little too sharply she thought. "What the hell do you mean I'm one adolescent?"

He snorted, shook his head. "Whatever," he said. "But that asshole come aroun' here, I bus' his chops 'kay?"

She laughed at that. "He's not like that, and besides, the guy is thirty-four."

"Yeah, what's with that?"

"What do you mean?"

"Fricken cradle robber."

She groaned at that one. "Jesus," she said to the ceiling, "why is it that certain guys think it's wrong for somebody my age to hang with someone ten years older? It would mean that he'd be fifty when I was forty. What's the big deal?"

"I don't care if da guy seventeen," Kimo said. "He puts you li'dis, he's a creep."

"Okay okay. I get it. Let's just drop this, okay?"

"'Kay."

After Kimo left, she went to the kitchen and dialed Mark's number, if anything to apologize to him for Kimo's stupid behavior, but she got his recording. So she went upstairs, and snorting at the stupidity of Kimo's presumptuous stance of sister-protection, she uncapped the bottle and took a long, hot slug of gin.

She stood in the room, looking into the closet. Lined up there were holokūs she had worn for piano recitals, and hanging there, at the end, was the blue one-piece bathing suit she wore when she and Herman had gone over the shallow water, he in the second seat from the back, she in the second from the front, and he taught her how to properly paddle. She felt a tingling in the skin on her sides, where he had placed his hands, their skin separated only by that thin layer of blue fabric, and remembered the brown skin of his chest, little patches of faint white where salt had dried there, which she tasted, again, on the tip of her tongue. A droplet of water had glistened in the base of the V of his collarbones above the muscles of his chest. The stepladder swayed. She held onto the top of it, the rope hard and prickly around her neck, the line from her neck to the beam coarse against her right cheek. Below on the dirt floor of the shed a cockroach scuttled across from a bag of manure to the truck. She saw the black knob of the gearshift through the dust-hazed window of the truck. She turned to look in the direction of the canoe, but it was too dark to see clearly, only the faint pale shapes of the orchids. Her heart hammered it her chest. She took two deep breaths, and then swayed sideways off the ladder, knocking it off its feet.

Danielle sat up. She put her hand to the top of her chest and felt the chain. "Twenty-four," she whispered. "Twenty-four." And within about eighteen hours she would be alone in this house, and twenty-four. She held the loop of hair between her thumb and forefinger, and whispered, "Twenty-four."

She was not sure if she had drifted off to sleep again or if time had simply passed without her knowing it, but it was light outside and she heard something metal rattling in the driveway, and then the gunning of an engine. She got up to go to the bathroom, and then put on denim shorts and a tanktop, took a long swig from the gin bottle and returned it to its place under the bed, and went downstairs to the front door. It was Donna, backing a trailer, complete with padded, U-shaped cradles, into the yard. She was having some trouble keeping it straight, and apparently wanted to back it right past the house and to the weeds next to the shed. The trailer itself was decked out with weeds, chunks of moss and vines dragging on the ground under it, and the tires looked low. Kimo came down the stairs carrying a large duffel bag.

"Eh," he said.

"When are you going?"

"Laters. Gimme a ride?"

"Sure." She watched him as he fiddled with the zippers, checked the contents. He was a great guy, really. And the fact that she felt a little twinge in the forehead, from just a little too much subsistence, made her feel bad. "Hey," she said. "Sorry about getting pissed yesterday. I know you're only trying to help."

He shrugged, then smiled at her. "'Kay."

"I appreciate it."

"It's just cause you my sister, 'kay?"

"Okay."

He looked out the window. "What da hell is she doing?"

"Trying to back a trailer up."

"Not. She's trying to fold it up."

"You got time to help us?"

"Yah. What you like do?"

"Get the canoe to the beach. Get it lashed, all that."

"Hayward can lash um." He came up closer, and Danielle held her breath and nonchalantly backed away, aware that he would be able to smell the gin.

When he went outside to talk to Donna, she went into the kitchen and got a glass of juice, squirted some around in her mouth, and swallowed it. Then she ate a banana and went back to the front door. Kimo was now backing the trailer up as Donna watched from the lawn, her arms folded, and this time it went straight, so that Danielle saw it slowly disappear to the side of the house, followed by the SUV, and then she heard the sounds coming in from the kitchen as he worked the trailer into the weeds next to the shed. When he was finished, he had the trailer parked at an angle, right near the canoe. They'd be able to try it out right away. Danielle decided to go out and say hello to Donna, but before she could, Donna spoke briefly to Kimo, looked at her watch, and then climbed into the SUV and drove off. Danielle snorted, looking at the empty road. She couldn't spare a minute? Well, Danielle didn't have time to chat anyway. Kimo had a plane to catch.

The airport was a seven-mile drive inland from Kaunakakai, and on the way Kimo explained what he would do: he could still call people from Honolulu about the escort boat, and he'd be home weekends. If you have any questions about anything, have one of the California girls talk to Hayward, because he'd paddled off and on for years. "I talk to Dad, too," he said, "tell 'im you're in the race. We'll be down when you come in. We get grinds an' stuffs, stake out one table at DeRussy Park."

"If we come in."

"Nah nah nah, don't think li'dat. When you come in."

"It might be dark by the time we get to eat, you know."

"Nah nah," he said. "You do fine."

At the airport Kimo leaned up to see if the concession place was open, which it was, and then turned and kissed her on the cheek. "'Kayden, take care ah?"

"Garans. An' you, no fall fo' haole girls ah? An' dakine—you mus' remembah not to dakine."

"Ho, let me write dat down. See you, let's see, this weekend, 'kay?"

He got out, pulled his duffel bag from the rear seat, and walked toward the low buildings, his body offset by the weight of the bag.

Donna took on the job of calling everyone to meet at Danielle's to load the canoe, and told Danielle that she thought The Airheads might be able to bring one or both of the Kama brothers to help, Hayward hopefully, so that he could help with the lashing. She, Tricia, Danielle, Marcia, and the long-lost Judy Beeman The Barf Queen waited for them, three of them out front while Tricia took Judy around back to show her the canoe and tell her the story of Herman Prince and Peggy MacNeil. The Airheads were still not there when they came back, Judy looking back again and again at the opening to the shed, then ahead with a skeptical expression on her face. "I don't know about this," she said. "I don't know if I like the idea of going in that particular canoe, although it looks what? Seaworthy? I guess that's the word."

"That's the word," Danielle said.

"But seaworthiness isn't what I'm thinking about. That is the canoe he lost in the card game. That is the shed it's been in, and that is the shed in which she committed suicide? I don't know." Then Judy looked off at something, and Danielle looked too. There was nothing there but clouds and the upslope of the mountain.

"Uh, what are you seeing there?" Danielle asked.

"Huh?" Judy looked at her, seeming confused by something. "Nothing," she said. "I was just—"

The Airheads pulled into the dirt driveway in Michelle's SUV. "Uh-oh," Donna said. "We're short a couple of Kamas. We can't do this."

"If we can get dakine to the beach," Danielle said, "then we can get somebody to dakine us with dakine so we can dakine."

The Airheads got out of their car and stopped before coming up the lawn. Something was wrong with them. "What's this?" Danielle asked.

"They look positively dowdy," Donna said.

They did—their hair wasn't right, their usual flashy clothes had been replaced by oversized tee shirts stained by water and mud, and they wore no jewelry. They came up the lawn, finger and toenails oddly pale.

"You guys look tired," Danielle said.

"Just more work with the fishponds," Chrissy said. "It's fun, kinda."

"We can't take the canoe out yet," Michelle said.

"Why?"

"Hayward said not to until it's blessed. He said, 'cannot paddle one canoe dat no mo blessed'. That's what he said."

"You mean like a kahuna?" Donna said. "Do we really have to do that? I mean, what year is this?"

"I'm not, like, going into any canoe that is no more like blessed okay?" Michelle got a weird look right after she spoke, as if she could not believe what she had just said. "I mean like—well, you know what I mean."

"So we get it blessed," Danielle said, trying to resist the impulse to laugh. Had she really said that? She looked around at the others. Nobody saw it as funny, and Judy was still staring at that mountain slope.

"He said he's gonna try getting his uncle to come up," Michelle said.

"When?"

"This afternoon, he said, but only like maybe. Like, fifty-fifty chance, so he was like, try get ready anyway. He said it would be good if we could give his uncle like fifty dollars or something, you know, just a, like, gifty thing?"

"We can do that," Donna said.

"He said we should clear that space around the canoe, like, cut more of the grass and stuff so that we can stand around it while the kahuna blesses the canoe."

Donna turned to Judy Beeman. "Would that make you feel more inclined? I mean if the canoe was properly blessed?"

"Maybe," she said. But she did not look convinced.

Mollie Teruya had apparently seen the crew behind the shed hacking away at the roots of the high grasses and carrying armloads to a pile off to the side. She came through the hedge with two dishes, one a lemon pie of some sort, and the other a plate of rolled sushi, the dark seaweed wrapped kind. Danielle introduced her to the parched, chaff-plastered workers she had not met yet, and explained what the gathering was for. Mollie wanted to know who the kahuna was, and Michelle said, "It's like, Corky Lee or Corky Wong or Corky Loo or something like that."

"Corky Liu!" Mollie Teruya said. "Know him long long long time. Mos' my life I guess." She thought a moment. "How many peoples hea laters?"

"About ten or so," Danielle said.

"'Kayden, I fix up choke eats fo you. Get turkey da freezah—stick um microwave, about ten, should feed. Ho, Corky Liu! I no see him ten twelve years. Ho, dis good fun."

"You sure this isn't an imposition on you?" Donna asked.

"What imposition? I cook, feed one grumpy o' man, t'row away da res'. I like whatchucall, one good race cah wit' nobody fo drive um."

Danielle knew she shouldn't do it, but while the crew worked at clearing space for the blessing, she used the pretense of going to the bathroom to go up to her room and take a slug of gin to keep her going. And when that ran low, she used the pretense of going to get some pupus downtown at Misaki's Grocery, and went to the Wines and Spirits store to get another bottle. She covered her tracks by bringing back chips and a case of Aloha Maid drinks. By the time Corky Liu was supposed to arrive, she had a little bit of a buzz on, feeling guilty about it but at the same time rationalizing that, considering the festive atmosphere of the gathering, this little lapse made sense.

By the time the Kama brothers arrived with Corky Liu, a little man who was very well dressed in slacks, black dress shoes, and an aloha shirt with pictures of palm trees and flowers on it, she was on that bleary thin line she knew well—she could function, talk, and do things without showing the state she was in, but she knew she was only just on the right side of the thin line, the other side of which was a giggling incoherence, a pulled-in dream. She observed Mollie and Corky Liu chatting as if what she observed were some cartoon, their movements and speech weird and dreamlike. She tried eating things to keep herself on the right side of the line—sushi, turkey that Mollie Teruya had thawed and brought up, chips and dip, even an Aloha Maid. So she was vaguely aware of the Kama brothers lashing the canoe and explaining that the ama had to be toed in just a little, that once it was lashed they would unlash the ama and 'iakos in one piece, mark the 'iakos so that they could be placed properly, so that at the beach it could be lashed again and would be ready to go.

She made one lucid observation about the Kama boys and The Airheads: as the brothers explained this and that about the lashing, Chrissy and Michelle watched and listened, and Danielle saw in the girls' bearing and facial expressions something so obvious that she instantly felt horribly envious—those girls were either in love or just short of it, and in so natural and legitimate and so clean a manner that she saw herself and Mark as a sick, random aberration, and she thought that if that situation had been her one chance, then the very cheapness of it identified her whole life as a dismal, ugly waste. She did not want to see it that way, and thought, or hoped, that she was wrong. She realized also that she still had time, not like Donna or Judy, who had given up and accepted their lives, or at least had seemed to.

Then she found herself standing in a circle around the canoe while Corky Liu walked around it with a wooden bowl and a ti leaf, sprinkling water on the hull and ama, and apparently chanting in Hawaiian. Then he stopped and looked around at the ten people surrounding it. "Hayward told me the story of this canoe," he said, "and it was amplified by Miss . . ." and he turned to Tricia, who whispered to him, ". . . by Miss Nakamoto. I have not heard this story before, although I have lived here all my life. This is a sad story and so this is a sad canoe. Canoes are sentient beings 'kay? In old times Hawaiians gave their canoes a kind of mind, and eyes, and memories. Canoes have histories, and this one, the *Keikiali'i*, has a sad history. With this blessing we restore it and make it fresh again, and get it ready to return to its element, which it has thirsted for almost a half a century. What you are doing is proper and important 'kay? Now I will continue." He turned again to the canoe, and when he did that, Danielle felt herself move over the line, but not to the giggling incoherence she was used to. She went over into a sensation of such horrible devastation and sadness that she was not sure she would be able to hold herself together. The girl who put the rope around her neck, the boy who promised to wait, Donna, Tricia, all of them, Danielle included, were nothing but frail packages of bones and flesh trying to stay on one side of a line, as Peggy MacNeil had tried to stay on one side of a line, and their chances were dim, because they were frail and weak and because life was so cheap, and because they had only a few years to experiment with being alive and circumstances made it such that they would fuck it up, over and over again, until they were dead. They all got their one chance, and for some reason some of them just couldn't take the idea seriously while they drank themselves to death or racked up their cars or overdosed or whatever. She was doing it again and knew it, and for some reason did not have any idea of how to stop herself.

Somewhere there the blessing was over, and she and the rest took pinches of pink sea salt and sprinkled them onto the hull of the canoe, after which she went to the house, muttering to Donna that she didn't feel that good, and went upstairs to the bathroom, locked the door, and threw up in the toilet, staring blearily at what she had eaten, fascinated by little strips of turkey skin, dark green seaweed from the sushi, and floating rice.

If there was anything good about that evening, it was that she slept as if knocked silly by a sandbag. In the middle of the night she was aware of the slapping of the corrugated metal on the roof, and it didn't affect her, as Kimo's absence didn't affect her.

She went back to sleep, and then woke up at seven a.m. with a headache and that sustained, subtle nausea she was familiar with, and which she countered with a slug of gin, this time in the kitchen, and put the bottle in one of the cabinets. She didn't have to hide it anymore. She ate her cereal with the sound of the automatic coffee maker gurgling and hissing in the background, and when it was done, took a cup outside. At the opening to the shed she stopped, and looked around at the pillow-shaped hunks of dried manure, the bags that held them rotted to the floor in tangles of burlap and plastic, and then at the old truck with its rusted tire rims in the dirt. It had regular tires in the nineteen-fifties, clear windows. She looked up at the beams spanning across, and the way the morning sun reflected off the parched weeds outside made the dusty, cobwebbed area under the roof more visible. She ran her eyes along the beams and at one place on the one right above her she stopped—it was something about the squared-off beam having a subtle interruption, a chafe mark, and she knew immediately that it was the beam from which Peggy MacNeil had hung herself. The rounded off half inch where the rope had been attached was still there, the rope having depressed the wood, perhaps worn it as the wind blew and made her body sway on the rope for some time before her mother came out of the house to discover it.

The nausea was back, and she wasn't sure if it was because of what she had seen or because of her hangover, but she poured the coffee out into the dirt, splattering warm mud droplets on her shins.

She walked back to the house with her hand gripped over her mouth, the hot, acidic liquids trying to force themselves out. When she was back in the kitchen the nausea went away, and she sat at the table breathing evenly until she felt reasonably functional again.

She slept in the late morning until the heat on the roof made the room too hot, and then got the idea that she might call Mark—it was late enough that he would be up, and she felt the need to talk. About what, didn't matter. She went down to the kitchen and dialed the number, and waited for the recording, but someone picked it up. "Yeah?" It was a dusky, sleepy woman's voice.

"Oh, sorry," she said. "I think I have the wrong number."

The woman just made a grunting sound and hung up.

Danielle went upstairs and sat on the bed. She looked out the window at Mollie Teruya's yard, and then felt the urge to cry, but instead ended up laughing and shaking her head. "So just what the hell did you expect?" she said. The silence of the room, and the heat, made her feel a strange sensation of isolation, as if there were no hard reality anymore, as if she were floating, a package of flesh and bones, a head with a brain in it, floating, almost as if there were no time. She was a random organism placed in a particular time, and her time might be twenty-five years or fifty years or a hundred, but at the same time it didn't matter. She was just an organism, and her life didn't mean much. She reached under the bed and drew out the bottle, uncapped it and took a slug, carefully swallowed, and then waited as the heat of the gin radiated down her trunk. "No," she said. "This is not nineteen-fifty. This is far from that."

She sat in the kitchen waiting for the late afternoon when they would come, and would load the canoe onto the trailer and take it down to Kaunakakai and the water. Donna knew a woman who lived on the beach, and said that they could leave the canoe parked in her yard, which fronted shallow water that was open enough that they could take it to the bay near the concrete pier. Corky Liu had said that it was a good thing they were doing, so she sat there and waited, so that they could get the canoe to its element. Whether or not racing it across the channel was a good idea rested in the back of her mind like a minor detail—to get the canoe to water was what Corky Liu had implied was the most important thing, but then, what was 'important'? Nothing was really important. Put the canoe wherever you feel like putting it. What difference did it make? If they bombed out where actually racing it was concerned, no problem. She now thought that they shouldn't do it—getting the canoe to the water would be enough, but the channel was too much. They didn't need to.

The lawn Donna had found to store the canoe on belonged to a Mrs. Baguio, whose husband sold real estate in Honolulu and came home on weekends. Their house was an old Hawaiian-style cottage with high ceilings and a roof with a double pitch, sharper in the middle and then angled more softly toward the eaves. The place was secure enough that they wouldn't have to worry about someone stealing the canoe, an idea Donna laughed at: "Where would you paddle it?" she asked.

It took only twenty minutes for Hayward to lash the booms to the hull, his hands working the ropes so that his forearms came alive, ropy with muscle that seemed to move like thick worms under his brown skin. Michelle and Chrissy watched with an almost devotional focus as he did this, and Donna turned to Danielle and whispered, "Whipped."

"I know. They just aren't themselves."

"I think I'm through poking fun at them."

"I know," Danielle said. "I know what you mean."

There were six of them this time, Marcia having some kid-oriented thing. In the powerhouse they would put Donna and Judy Beeman, sitting two and five would be The Airheads, Tricia would steer, and Danielle would take the stroke position. While they worked at slowly easing the canoe into the water, Danielle looked forward and then back, at its shape, and where before she had thought it looked tubby, now she thought it looked almost sleek, the looping 'iakos dark and the ama some kind of wood lighter colored than koa. Wiliwili, one of the Kama boys had called it. Hayward had fashioned two sawed-off Clorox bottle bailers, twine tied from their finger loops to the 'iako lashing.

Danielle sat in seat one, her stomach starting to bother her again with that vague nausea. She had taken another couple of swigs of gin before coming down, and thought that it would switch the nausea off, but as soon as she positioned herself on the seat, the wind chilling her wet legs and lower body, she began to suspect that it would get worse. Strenuous physical activity usually turned it off, though, and she grabbed the paddle, held it over the water, and waited. "Okay," Michelle called, and then called, "Hit!" and they were off, the little coralheads, rocks, and seaweed sweeping under the hull. Danielle tried to set a medium pace, just to get a feel for the canoe, and Michelle called the hut-hut-ho every sixteenth stroke. Just as they made it to slightly deeper water, Danielle stroking evenly and trying to fight the nausea that seemed to grow as she paddled, the canoe heaved sideways and dumped her over into the water.

They caught the 'iakos before the canoe went belly up, and pushed back until the ama slapped the water and the canoe was upright again. "Sorry!" Tricia called from the other end. "Sorry! My fault!" Danielle stood in the water, up to her chest, and held the front of the canoe while the others worked with the bailers and their hands to get the water out. She touched the top of her chest and felt the chain, then felt herself beginning to shiver, the nausea swelling in her trunk. "I don't feel good," she said.

"We get out in the water," Donna said. "You'll shake it off."

"Okay."

Four paddled while Judy and Donna bailed. Practice. They'd probably huli the canoe in the race, so she figured they'd better get their bailing technique together. Danielle tried to hold the pace but felt miserable, sick, almost as if she had gotten the flu. By the time they made the bay, she was hunched over most of the time, moaning down between her knees at the water sloshing in the bottom of the hull, forward, then back, forward, then back.

They finally made it back to the little beach fronting Mrs. Baguio's lawn, and without the help of Hayward, managed to half-carry and half-drag the canoe up onto the lawn. Danielle sat down in the grass, her arms around her trunk. The rest milled about for a few minutes, some guzzling water from bottles they had left near a tree, others wandering around looking at the plants. Gradually they reassembled near Danielle, sitting in the grass and resting, except for Judy, standing down near the beach staring, again along the shoreline.

"You okay?" Donna asked.

"Yeah. No. What's with Judy? She's gonna bag on us, is that it?"

Donna looked at her and shrugged. "Beats me," she said, "and no, I asked her more than once about that. She says she wants to go." She turned back to Danielle. "But we've gotta practice changes, we've gotta practice endurance, we've gotta do all kinds of stuff, and we don't really want to iron this race with you doubled over in the escort boat. We don't even have the other three paddlers."

"I know."

"I'm working on that," Tricia said. "I'm e-mailing the world."

The others looked on, waiting for more. Danielle didn't care.

"It means that gin and paddling don't mix," Donna said. "You'll be dehydrated all the time. It robs you of your strength."

"I know."

"Should we continue with this? It's your canoe, I know, but—"

"No." Now she was beginning to get irritated. "No, I can do it."

"Because you're hurting yourself."

"That's what my dad said."

"We'll help," Michelle said.

She looked at Michelle, thinking, you little bitch, I don't need your help. You airhead, you dismal bimbo. "Let's just wait a minute here," she said. "I don't think that it's up to you to decide what I'm doing with myself. It's none of your business."

"Sorry," Michelle said. "All we said is we'd help." She looked at Chrissy, who looked down, and then away.

"I don't need anybody's help, you get that?"

"Yup, like I got it," Michelle said.

"And you don't need to soup it up with that valley girl stuff either."

"Sorry," Michelle said, but the expression on her face was jaunty, seemed to Danielle almost aggressive.

"Fuck you," Danielle said. "When I need help I'll ask for it."

Donna cleared her throat. "Look—"

"You're not my mother," Danielle said. "I paddle as hard as anybody." She held her hand up. "That's a blister, sister."

There was an odd, airy silence after that, and she thought, did I really say that? No one laughed. She could tell that they wanted to laugh. Tricia stared, eyes shifting from one person to another.

"Oh shit," Danielle said.

"Okay," Donna said. "I'm not your mother. So that's settled."

"I can take care of myself."

"Okay."

She was calming down, and now felt mortified at her behavior. She should apologize to Michelle. She wanted to, but couldn't make herself do it. She couldn't even look at her.

"You want to stay at my place for a while?" Donna asked.

"No, it's all right. I'll behave."

She was not sure why she did it, and thought that it might just be the idleness of sitting around in the morning that caused it, but she found herself staring up at the beam in the old shed, trying to see those notches, and then looked around in the shed for a ladder. There was a stepladder, and she wondered if it could be the ladder that Peggy MacNeil had used, and decided that it was probably not. The ladder looked new, so she set it up, and climbed the dusty rungs until she was high enough to reach the beam, and when she got there, steadying herself by holding onto the beam, she went up one more step so that her eyes were nearly level with the parched, dark wood. There between her hands gripping the beam, was the rounded off notch. She felt behind, on the other side, and there was another notch. Then she looked down. Between her feet on the rung and the dirt was a space of about five feet. This was the last thing Peggy MacNeil had seen, this perspective from up on a ladder, probably a rickety wooden ladder that must have been removed from the shed after her suicide, maybe Mei's doing because the old woman would not have wanted that particular ladder in the shed. The rope, too. She scanned the junk in the shed looking for rope, and saw none. They would have removed it because it was evidence, or at least Mei would have gotten rid of it. She looked up again at the notch, and visualized the rope going over it, then visualized the squeaking sound it must have made when weight was put on it, maybe a shudder from the old building itself as the body hung under the beam, swaying back and forth in a decreasing pendulum until it was still. A twenty-four-year-old girl who had decided that this was the best way to respond to her circumstances, and standing there on the rung, Danielle felt herself going into a strange sensation of identification with that girl, as if she herself were becoming that girl, as if her hair was now black and her facial features had gone through a metamorphosis, as if she were now in possession of every memory of that girl, the taste of salt on her tongue, the broad chest of Herman Prince, the sensation of his hands on her sides that she would not feel again, and she felt the coarse rope around her neck, and visualized the act of pushing her feet sideways to upend the ladder, then the short drop she made until the rope closed violently around her neck, and she reached up to grab it in the sound of the ladder crashing to the dirt below, only to find that the rope was buried too far in the flesh for her fingers to do anything about it, encircling her neck and feeling as hard as an iron bar, the knot pinching her skin and her chest beginning to heave with convulsions while she scratched vainly at the skin of her neck. What would she have seen then? Swinging, perhaps rotating on the end of the rope, she would have seen the open doors of the shed admitting a square plane of faint light that came from the kitchen window of the house, perhaps even heard the sound of pots and pans bonging as her mother washed them in the sink, and then, rotating slowly around and swinging, shocked by the pain with her face feeling increasingly bloated as if the veins on her forehead might burst, and feeling the fading desperation for air changing into a sweeping relaxation as she allowed her hands to drop to her sides in an acceptance of the oblivion she wanted, she would see the faint shapes of bags of manure, pots, and finally from her elevated perspective, her consciousness beginning to leave her, a brightening line of orchids, seven of them intensifying out of the darkness until they were all as luminous as if lit by powerful sunlight, brilliant in their color, all in bloom in pinks, yellows, and purples.

Sometimes there were only five paddlers, sometimes seven, one waiting on the beach while six went out on short runs. Her outburst made practice tense for Danielle, but she got the impression from Michelle's bearing, pretty much all business, that the incident had been more or less forgotten. At times she wanted to stop and say something to her, but either she diplomatically avoided Danielle or simply had forgotten the whole thing. She asked Donna about it, and Donna said that it was no biggie—just a brief catfight, nothing to worry about. But Danielle did worry about it, and felt a peculiar alienation from the rest of them because of it. But business is business, and she tried to concentrate on the paddling.

The next problem had to do with Judy. Donna said that she was waffling, as if she were planning to bag the race but didn't want to tell them. If she did, then they'd have only nine paddlers, even assuming Tricia could produce for them. It had to do, Donna said, with Honolulu paranoia, not so much toxins as her former husband. Donna had talked to her and she had seemed doubtful.

After a practice that Judy was not in on, Danielle asked about her. "Keep your fingers crossed," Donna said, squirting her paddle off with the garden hose. She handed it to Danielle.

"The last three times I've seen her she's been locked in the middle distance stare, always looking—" Danielle squirted her paddle and gestured at the beach with her head.

"Yeah," Donna said. "You notice the direction? The west end. That's where we turn the corner for the channel."

"But didn't she say that it was a long time ago? I mean, she's been here for years."

Donna shook her head. "I don't know. I can't seem to get a straight story from her."

Tricia's advertising began to pay off: she got an on-off paddler from Honolulu that she had gone to high school with, a freshman division regatta paddler who finally bit when she absorbed the story of Herman Prince and Peggy MacNeil, and Tricia was working on two more, all with her e-mail. Why not just call? Donna asked her, and she told them that in this case text worked better—they could think while they read without the distraction of a phone to the ear. Her name was Kathy Shimabukuro, and she had done change races before. She would show up mid-week before the race. Garans. The only problem was that she wasn't in good enough shape to do the channel. But then, Tricia said, we're not in it to win, only to take Herman Prince's canoe across.

Danielle cut down the gin to one sip in the morning, and felt better. But as they continued to practice, she realized that even that one sip was stealing something from her. It had to be none at all, so it became none, and she thought, hell, when it's over I can go back to the Wines and Spirits store and get more—this is just a leave of absence. No problem.

But she discovered, over the days of practice, that when she got up in the morning and sat in the empty house eating her cereal and banana and juice, she had a feeling of a strange wholeness, as if she had had the flu for six years and was now just emerging from the state of half-irritated grogginess and the physical malaise that went with being sick. She spent parts of the days out in the back, hacking down the tall grasses, watering the orchids lined along Mollie Teruya's hedge, even trying to deal, garbage bag by garbage bag, with the junk in the shed, passing under that beam with the soft notch in it sometimes without thinking that she was passing under the beam from which Peggy MacNeil hung herself. It was true, too, that she knew she was doing this only as a leave of absence, yet the idea of a permanent leave itself slowly emerged as a possibility, as if some strange replacement were occurring, one state of mind for another—like a photographic negative being tipped to the light so that everything that was dark took on a silvery sheen and everything bright became dark. In a way it confused her because it was no more than an experiment she was carrying out, with her surprised but skeptical every morning, as if the experiment would have to bomb out sooner or later.

Controlling the alcohol made her a little anxious in the evenings, and three evenings in a row she tried to call Donna and the phone was busy. It was busy when she tried an hour later on each of those evenings, and she began to worry about Donna, but each day Donna showed up for practice looking more or less normal. Those times when she heard the busy tone, or got no answer, were the worst—she jiggled her knee, looked again and again at the door, thinking, what the hell, just go get a bottle. But she would shake it off, thinking, this is an experiment.

A week before the race, the problem of the escort boat became urgent. They couldn't put it off any longer. Kimo wasn't even coming back weekends, so Danielle couldn't pester him about it. But he had said it was garans, so she took the chance and trusted him. Tricia did her magic with two more paddlers, both of whom would come mid-week along with Kathy Shimabukuro. Garans. As for their conditioning, they too would spend more time in the escort boat than in the canoe, but that was no problem. Tricia would steer, and iron the race except for one change in calmer water if someone else wanted to try steering. That left nine to man the five seats. So the escort boat was the last obstacle. Some of the girls had asked around, Hayward had asked around, but either they just weren't getting lucky with it or so many boats were already committed that there were none left that could make the channel, or at least none left with the proper insurance and size. When she drove down to Kaunakakai each day to practice, she would see boats in yards, but they would all appear to be in storage more than anything else, whatever colors they had bleached faint by the sun, their hulls mildewed or dusty.

One night when she was at Donna's place, while Donna seemed to have lapsed into some bummed-out reverie, or at least some speculative reverie, Danielle couldn't tell, she asked her if she could use the phone to call Kimo. "He'd probably be home by now."

"Sure, go ahead."

"I mean if it's all right. Would you rather I did this later?"

"No, it's okay," Donna said, in an uncharacteristically pleasant voice. "I was just thinking, that's all."

"Me too. I've been thinking a lot."

"We're all up on our ladders with nooses around our necks," Donna said. "Why we put ourselves up there is what I'd like to know."

Danielle felt her face flush. "What makes you think it was a ladder?"

"What else would it have been?" She sat up, then shook her head, then came out with an amiable snort. "Your options go this way, and they go that way," she said. "It's interesting." Danielle stared at her, and she shook her head again, and laughed, waving her hands before her as if she were convinced she had been misinterpreted. "Never mind. Go ahead and call."

She dialed the number he had given her, of an apartment he was sharing with a couple of other guys. He answered.

"It's the escort boat," she said. "We're having trouble getting one."

"Eh, good you remind me of that. Hang on a sec, I ask."

"Ask who?" But he was already off the phone.

She waited for a full two minutes before he picked it up again. "We come."

"Who's we?"

"Me an' Keoni," he said.

"Keoni Hong?"

"Yah. Two days ago I asked him. Just making sure."

"You mean he's not in jail? I mean he should be."

Kimo laughed. "Nah nah—they put him in college. Try chance one alternative punishment yah? One special therapeutic measure. He can use his uncle's boat. Get killer outboards underneath. What, fifty horses? I dunno."

"You guys'll get bombed and forget. You'll go to Maui instead and say, 'chee, wheah da fricken race? What, dey cancel um?'"

"Nah nah nah, we no fo'get."

"Garans?"

"Put um inna bank."

"I'm gonna call you every night for five nights before the race 'kay? Because if you don't make it here, we're toast."

"Then this is the first night."

Was it? She looked at Donna, who still stared into space, as if she were thinking out some cryptic philosophical question.

"Is it? I guess it is."

"No worries," he said. "We come—ho, blast across da channel. Good fun. Keoni's done it before too, the men's race, no worries. It's twenty-four feet long, get insurance, get one authentic radio, and all li'dat. He knows da routine."

"I see disaster lurking in the wings."

"Nah, garans babes. No mo worries."

When she hung up, she felt hot. Keoni Hong was as close to a blathering street person as any of Kimo's friends she knew. Even if they did make it, he would be stinking of pakalōlō and beer. She was convinced at that moment that this would be a disaster. Those two would not show, and they would not go. End of story.

"I've got a boat," she said. "I think."

"Really," Donna said, and then stared again into the middle distance before her. Then she seemed to shake herself out of it, and laughed again. "Oh, really," she said. "Yeah, that's good. So it's on."

Sunday morning of the last week of September, Danielle woke up in a tent, unable for five seconds to figure out why she was there. She reached up and felt the loop of hair on the chain. It was still dark, and she rolled herself a little, bumping into Donna, who groaned in her sleep and began to snore. She pulled the tent zipper up a little, and saw, faintly, the raw shoreline of Hale O Lono Harbor, boats beyond it, and then she heard the hissing sound of water sweeping up over sand. When she squinted again into the darkness, she saw the elliptical shape of the rear manu of the *Keikiali'i* against the dark sky, a light-colored mast pole beyond it swaying so that it peeked away from one side of the manu and then the other. She sat up and looked around, and saw the little digital clock Donna had brought along tied to the top of the arced tentpole. Five a.m. Kimo had called Donna's cellphone the previous evening to inform her that he and Keoni were going to 'check out Lahaina first, den come. Garans—we see you laters 'kay?' Danielle had taken the phone and had gone through the usual conversation: you won't make it—you'll get bombed and sleep until ten. You'll forget which direction to go. But he simply laughed. Nah nah nah. Cool yoa jets babe.

She lay back down again, and pulled the sleeping bag flap over her shoulder. In the other three tents the rest slept, in a bigger one Tricia and The Debutantes. Danielle knew that it was in a way unfair to call her friends that. They were Japanese girls who clearly had done some paddling in their lives—darker skin and good shoulders, all three of them pretty and reserved, but there was no question about the shape of their bodies, that hint of strength from the waist up.

She was shaken awake by Marcia later, and the tent was heating up, light glowing through the blue nylon. She crawled out and saw Tricia and Judy working on the old tarp, or spray skirt, covering the hull, a zip-hole for each seat. Or at least Tricia was working. Judy made faint gestures at leaning over to help, and then stood up and looked west along the shoreline. Tricia was pouring baby oil on the zippers and opening and closing them. Danielle looked around for a Port-a-Potty, which she saw too far away, and decided to go stand in the water. Number Two would be a little later, after they ate. The harbor had a small opening, and the interior formed a rough circle, with only one coarse sand beach, and all the escort boats were lined along the circular shore. Donna stood out on the rocks with her arms folded, looking out to the left, toward Kaunakakai. Danielle knew right away what the problem was. It was six-fifteen, and Kimo had not shown yet. Now Donna had the cellphone to her ear. Who would she be calling?

Maybe trying to get another boat? When Danielle got there, Donna folded the cellphone up and put it in the pocket of her parka.

"No sign of them," she said.

"I knew it," Danielle said. "I just knew it."

The ocean in the direction of Kaunakakai looked choppy, and the only boats in the harbor were ones they had seen the day before. The officials' tent had a little crowd of paddlers around it, some holding up tee shirts, some leaning over tables talking with people seated behind them. Out past the harbor opening she could just see one of the orange buoys with the rope suspended across, the starting line. Donna kept staring in the direction of Kaunakakai. "Tricia's doing all the details," she said. "We're number sixty-two. There are six koas in the race. Sixty-five canoes in all."

"Sixty-four. Fricken Kimo."

"Is he trustworthy?"

"Yeah, except for when he hangs around criminals. Shit. I knew this would happen." She looked back at the parking area. All the elaborate preparations, put your stuff in waterproof bags, make your arrangements, we'll do this, the Kama brothers'll do that, we'll pick you up when you come back. She felt a rush of horrible embarrassment. She should have known. All the trouble they had gone through—all the way down to the long, dusty ride out here, all for nothing.

She ate, she used the Port-a-Potty, she stretched. Six-forty-five. Now the rest began whispering to each other, looking out at the ocean. Once, Danielle sat down and put her face in her hands, and had to fight like hell to keep from crying. She would never forgive him, never. Then it seemed as if it was ordained that they would not go across. She stood on the rocks with Donna, staring until her head began to ache. There were spots on the horizon that melted into nothing, there were canoes already in the water, crews warming up outside the harbor opening.

"I knew it," Danielle said. "Shit. Sometimes I think with him there's like a screw loose somewhere. Damn."

Donna leaned a little forward, as if the ten inches closer to the horizon would give her better vision. "Hmm, maybe only an optical illusion," she said. "Or something out there."

Danielle looked. Maybe. It was like a peculiar, undulating shape on the horizon, not a wave.

"Thar she blows," Donna said.

A blue boat materialized on the horizon, flying parallel to the shore, about four hundred yards out, clearing the waves and then slamming down and sending up fans of spray behind it, the delayed sound of a kind of metallic thumping, an unsynchronized drumbeat coming across the water.

"Gotta be," Danielle said.

The boat slowed down sharply once it approached the harbor opening, its own wake washing forward and raising its stern, and moved slowly into the harbor toward the officials' tent. Danielle squinted at the figures inside until she saw one climb down into the water—Kimo, no question.

Tricia appeared next to her. "Is that them?" she whispered.

"That's them."

Tricia took a deep breath, and then let it out. "Okay," she said. "That's it. Can I ask you guys to come over here? Everyone else is there, too. I want to say something."

"How come is it that you've talked more in the last month than you've probably ever talked in your life?" Danielle asked.

She giggled, and then cut it off as usual. "I don't know," she said. "I'm trying to get used to—" She stopped, something seeming to have occurred to her. Then she looked suddenly frightened, even mortified. "I—" She shook her head. "No, I just want to say something." She went back toward the others.

Danielle looked at Donna, who held her shoulders up in a sustained shrug. "There she goes again," she said.

"It's only a race," Danielle said.

"No, it's something else bothering her. She's been weirder than her usual weird lately. But hey, let's get ready."

The object of the gathering was the distribution of nine little gold chains, each with a coil of hair perfectly tied off with thin sugi, one for each of the paddlers minus Danielle, who already had hers, and which, she realized, looked somewhat crude compared to Tricia's jeweler's perfection in the execution of the loops. Tricia went into a little speech, which sounded rehearsed to Danielle, in which she said that these were loops of Peggy MacNeil's hair, and for luck, they were going to wear them across the channel.

Judy Beeman had seemingly been only half listening until she heard that. "This strikes me as a little ghoulish," she said. "Thanks, but I don't know about this. In fact, I don't know at all about—" She looked at the harbor.

"Did you take more Bonine?" Donna asked.

"Yes," she said, a doubtful expression on her face. They had convinced her to take the anti-nausea pill the previous evening, and she did so. She had taken another in the morning. "That's a good try at changing the subject, but there's something a little sick about this."

"Did you ever have a rabbit's foot?" Tricia asked her.

"Yes, when I was a little girl," Judy Beeman said. "Why?"

"Did you realize that it was the foot of a rabbit?"

"Well, yes, I suppose."

"It was cut off a rabbit," Tricia said. "A rabbit's foot is the foot of a rabbit. It's bones, dried muscle and skin, and fur and nails. If you take one and kind of scratch it on the skin, you can actually smell a faint kind of decomposition. It is the foot of a rabbit. Then you wonder, which foot? Front right—"

"That's like, gross," Michelle Forten said.

"Which is more gross?" Tricia asked, "one of these hairs, or the foot that was chopped off a rabbit?"

"Okay," Judy Beeman said, squinting at the little circular clasp. "I get the point."

"That guy," one of The Debs said. Her name, Danielle thought, was Nikki or something. "You know his name?"

"Which one? The one with Kimo?" Danielle asked. She nodded. "His name is Keoni Hong."

"Keoni Hong!" she said. "I went school with him."

"Me too," Kathy Shimabukuro said, and then the two of them looked at each other with what appeared to be dawning horror, or at least appalled disbelief.

"He's reformed," Danielle said. "He's in college."

"Not," Nikki said. "Cannot be. Nah, wrong guy."

"So, who's shark bait?" Donna asked.

Shrugs, looks.

"Impossible," Donna said. "Somebody's lying."

"No boddah me," Nikki said.

Danielle was halfway between periods, and that made her think briefly of Mark, who, for some reason, felt to her as remote as a junior high boyfriend. And with that thought, she wondered if it would ever happen, if she would ever experience what Donna said she'd had three years of. She stood holding her paddle and stared at the others. Maybe never, maybe next week. Didn't matter now.

They were about to break up to make their own preparations when Judy cleared her throat loudly and said, "Okay, I have to say something too, since people think they have to say things before races."

Tricia giggled, then seemed to cringe.

"Okay," Donna said doubtfully.

"I'll say it once," Judy went on. She touched the loop of hair at her throat. "My husband isn't in Honolulu. He's in Los Angeles. I've been on the phone with him for a couple of days now."

"Well, that's good," Donna said. "I mean—"

Judy held up her hand. "I'm not finished. Fourteen years ago I shot him." She looked around. Danielle looked away and cringed, and caught the same expression on Marcia's face. "I know," Judy went on. "It's true that I was abused, but the circumstances under which I did it are—well, ambiguous. He used to point his .22 at me sometimes and philosophize. He'd say, 'I could shoot you now I suppose, but what would that mean? Nothing, most likely, because existence itself is absurd, life is no more than blah blah blah.' We were high and argued, and so I picked up the gun, laughing and nodding, and said, 'I could shoot you blah blah,' and pointed it at him, and he had this superior, dismissive look on his face so I pulled the trigger. Amazing—he actually got an expression, like, indeed, why did you do that? Then he held his shoulder and seemed to understand that I had just tried to kill him, and nothing was so meaningless anymore and he started screaming and called the police." She snorted, and then looked out toward the western end of the island. "There's an outstanding warrant for my arrest for attempted murder."

"Okay," Donna said.

"He thought I did it on purpose and reported it that way. As I told you, he's very superior, or was. Everybody was an idiot but him. I was an idiot too. So I shot him. Then when he understood that he wasn't a genius in a world of morons, he tried to rescind the warrant, or something, but the State of California doesn't just throw warrants away. But I was already gone. It was like, good riddance. He has a little scar on his left shoulder," and she touched herself there, "to remember me by."

The listeners looked at one another. "Well," Danielle said, then looked at Donna.

"He's been alone all these years, as I have," Judy said. "Apparently I'm the only moron he could live with."

Tricia produced an uneasy, truncated laugh. Judy looked at her. "I know," she said. "So I'm going to talk to him. He's coming from California. Not today though. Tuesday."

"And the warrant?" Donna asked.

"I'm thinking about that. I think I might go talk to someone."

"That might be good," Donna said.

"It might. I want it over with." She snorted and looked out toward the west end of the island. "He doesn't sound like the pompous jerk he used to be. If I were to talk to him, I wonder if any of you would mind meeting him."

"Of course," Donna said.

"Sure," Danielle said. She looked around. The rest nodded and came out with affirmative shrugs.

"He sound's almost—" Judy looked at the bay. "Almost tolerable," she said. "On the phone he—" She stopped, looking almost stricken. "He said he'd go with me wherever we had to go and he'd do what he could to get that warrant—overturned, or something—some legal term. I don't know."

"Well," Donna said, "you got guts."

"I'll second that," Danielle said.

"Me three," Marcia said.

"Thanks," Judy said. "I don't have guts really. I still have to call when we get there, because he doesn't know where I am, exactly. The idea is scary. So I'm going to face the music in a koa canoe." She thought, staring at the bay. "I thought about that. I know I'll probably barf my guts out before we get halfway, but I thought finally that it was the reason I decided to do this. It's like the idea of it wouldn't let me chicken out." She looked at her watch. "Speaking of which," she said. "Look, I don't want this to change anything, okay?"

"Roger," Donna said.

Kimo and Keoni Hong came toward them, Kimo waving, and Tricia moved away from the group and talked to them, pointing back toward the pile of gear at their former campsite. Then they went to gather up the waterproof bags and plastic garbage bags full of clothes changes, handbags, and food, to take to the escort boat. Kimo saw Danielle and waved, called, "See you odda side 'kay?"

"Eh, tanks ah?" she called.

There was nothing left to do but get ready, and the only question left was whether or not the race would go, because the sky to the south was heavy with clouds, and Tricia came back with information that there were showers predicted, and that the seas were not exactly pacific, as you might expect. Danielle ignored the information and found herself experiencing something she hadn't in a long time—a buzz of nervousness that hadn't attacked her in years. She had to wade into the water twice more, she felt the thumping of her heart, felt it in her neck, and she had a hard time holding her hands still, something she had felt as a teenager before a race but had not felt in years, because in the past few years when she paddled she approached races with a placid, passive amiability that one would call a seasoned state of being 'cool'. The gin had guaranteed that, had dulled or drugged out any normal or honest anxiety she might have felt. Now she was both eager and badly frightened, as if she had regressed into being a novice.

Danielle would stroke for the first forty-five minutes. Michelle would sit two and call changes, loud enough to compensate for being slightly out of position for calling changes, Marcia and Judy would sit three and four, Judy saying that her best chance was to be in the canoe rather than in the escort boat with those babooze hotdogs. Nikki, the strongest of The Debutantes, would sit five, and Tricia, who wanted to iron the race with maybe one rest if they got to calmer waters, would steer. She had a camelback for water, and three granola bars lined up under the band of her bathing suit bottom. Kimo would let them know when they were clear for a change.

The nervousness Danielle had felt on shore transformed itself into a sensation of being bloated with energy, her heart banging in her neck and her hands firm on the paddle, the circle of old canvas holding her shirt against her waist. She remembered this from the old days—the nervousness was just the body waking itself up, and as they paddled out toward the start line, Tricia and Marcia talked in a near shout about where they should position themselves, and decided on the middle. Their theory was to approach Diamond Head and cut an inside line for the buoy. Outside lines in unpredictable water were, well, unpredictable, but an inside line wasn't—it was risky because the swells might be bigger, but you'd get occasional rides before standing still in the huge backwashes.

They paddled to the harbor opening and, after making their way through a little traffic jam of colorful canoes, they were out on the open water. It seemed as if there had to be more than sixty-five canoes. The brightly colored Bradleys and Force-Fives moved into position, and Danielle pulled toward an opening, only to have it closed by someone else. To their right they could see two koas, together, Lanikai and let's see, Outrigger probably. The others were farther to their left. Next to them was a flat green and white Lanikai Force-Five, the girls all wearing white long-sleeve shirts and sporting baseball caps, the stroker with a blonde ponytail coming through the gap in back. She was pretty and had that V-shaped upper body, and lanky as she was, Danielle knew that she was probably stronger than anyone in the *Keikiali'i*. The girl turned and waved, for what reason Danielle didn't know, but she waved back anyway. "Lanikai," Michelle said. "They'll blow us out of the water."

"The Australians here? The Rigaroos?"

"I don't know. Probably. It's Offshore California that'll blow everybody out of the water."

"What are we called?"

Michelle thought a moment. "We're like, The Clockwise Amas."

She didn't get it at first, and then laughed. "That's us," she said. "We are the Clockwise Amas." She looked back at Michelle. "Listen," she said, "about that blow-up of mine—"

Michelle shook her head. "No," she said, "we all knew you needed to do that. You got much better after that."

"Yeah but—"

"No, no problem," she said, and then laughed. "'That's a blister, sister.'"

"I can't believe I said that."

"You know," Michelle said more softly, "we think we got problems? I'm a little scared for Judy."

"I am too," Danielle said.

The officials' boat crossed before them a hundred-fifty yards out, some of the escort boats off to the side and waiting for the start, others still emerging from the harbor opening. And the start happened without much fanfare—the long hollow blat of a horn, and they began pulling, Danielle setting a vigorous stroke and concentrating ahead, aware that the Lanikai canoe had swept ahead like an arrow and was already a canoe length ahead, then one and a half, the blonde stroker setting a pace that put them ahead of everyone Danielle could see.

As the harbor edge receded and the wind coming from the southeast began to pick up, she pulled, reversed the stroke when they got the call at sixteen or eighteen strokes, and in the plane of her peripheral vision she was aware of the various colored lines of other canoes all pointing toward an empty spot on the horizon, toward which the dark projection of the Keikiali'i's manu aimed. She could hear, behind them, the multitude of boat engines revving, but they would stay back for a half an hour or more. The chop on the water was not bad, slapping across the nose and fanning sometimes off the

V-shaped pale kai, which deflected it off to the side. Still, she felt water begin to slosh at her feet.

Gradually, the shore of Moloka'i began to recede off their right shoulders, and they went into the open water, the southeast wind stronger against their left sides. "No sunburn!" someone yelled. True, it was overcast, and the dark clouds south of the island chain seemed to have moved toward them rather than away. Ahead they saw, interspersed here and there, vanishing and then appearing in the swells, some of the other canoes. She caught a glimpse of one ahead of them that was koa.

Hold the pace—she now felt a familiarity with it and was able to concentrate exclusively on the motion of her body, no rocking or lunging, just the sweep of the water and the sensation of sockets and bones and muscles moving something like a machine, with the same angles and forces reproduced in each stroke, something everyone else in the canoe must have felt, because the canoe did not bounce. Rhythm, balance, and power. The manu stayed there before her despite the swells, almost as if nailed into one spot, Moloka'i off their right shoulders. They would not see their escort boat until they reached Lā'au Point at the channel edge.

But then the water changed. Apparently they were entering an area where the edge of the channel swells affected the water, and the boat heaved up and then nosed into water and heaved up again, and a tongue of water swept right over the nose of the canoe, and then it was as if they had stopped. Someone had stopped paddling. Danielle turned and saw Marcia turned, and then beyond her Judy bailing while Marcia fiddled with the canvas. "Keep paddling," Tricia yelled. "You can't stop!"

They went back to it, and just as Danielle turned to continue the stroke she saw ahead, in one bizarre flash, an ama go up and over. "Oops, huli," Michelle said. "Gotta steer right." Tricia had seen it and steered right. The way the waves were coming, steering left might have flipped the canoe. They passed the paddlers in the water, at the same time hearing the gunning of an escort boat engine behind them. The women were working on getting a yellow canoe back over, and they passed within fifty feet. Another motor behind them gunned, and then the sound came up to their side, fifty feet to the right. Kimo. He leaned out over the gunnel, his hands cupped around his mouth. "Okay?" he called.

Danielle nodded, and they pulled ahead. Then they were in bigger swells, some that looked so huge that she imagined they would be swamped before going over, and the canoe rose into one, its manu way up, a dark silhouette in the sky, and then she felt something like the sensation of going over the top of a roller-coaster as it went down again, steered sharp to the right by Tricia, who had to do that in order not to flip, and then another swell came at them and blasted over the pale kai and into Danielle's face so that she was blinded for a moment, but kept paddling. She shook her head and looked and kept stroking, the paddle sometimes catching air, and out there, in the distance, she caught sight of other canoes rising and then nosing down, and another large swell came at them and pushed the canoe to the left, Tricia holding the rear end against flipping, and then they went backwards she thought, before having their rear end tipped up so high that the horizon vanished out of sight at the top of her eyes as the nose went under and then came up again, with one dreamlike flash on the horizon, of an ama rolling over in a rapid, perfect half-circle, like a dial. Once they were level she sensed forward movement, and the canoe seemed to zoom off, leaning her back, and ahead were two canoes both upside down, the paddlers swimming around, their paddles in their fists. They were too close together, but Danielle assumed that Tricia had already seen them, and kept paddling as the canoes slowly turned in the water, tossed by the swells, and she increased the pace, expecting Tricia to turn the canoe, and then she realized that Tricia was going between them, and she pulled as hard as she could, saying with each stroke, "Oh God, oh God, oh God," and the canoe shot forward on a wave as the ama of one and the nose of another swept past on either side, one of the paddlers in the water letting out a whoop of exhilaration. Once they were free, another huge swell getting ready to elevate their nose to a forty-five degree angle, Danielle dug her paddle in and pulled with all she had, screaming, "I love this! I love this!"

Her left buttock became numb just before the first change. Kimo called from fifty feet to their right, who's resting? Danielle raised her paddle, and she heard Judy call, and then Michelle. Keoni took the boat fifty yards ahead, and she saw three girls go off the side, Donna, Chrissy Moore, and a Deb, and they lined up according to their seats, Chrissy Moore the furthest away because she would stroke. The three of them waved their arms and slapped the water to make sure they could be seen. Tricia aimed the canoe as they paddled toward them, and when the heads bobbed up and down twenty feet ahead, Danielle unzipped a little to give herself room to slide out, put the paddle forward into the hollow nose of the canoe, and rolled off the right side. The water felt warm, and Donna bobbed in it, looking at her—you okay? Yup, fine, and Donna struggled herself up into the seat left by Judy Beeman. Chrissy Moore took the stroke-seat.

Once the canoe was off again, the paddles flashing in the flat light, Keoni brought the boat about so that they could climb up the aluminum ladder.

As soon as she was under the blue tarp and latched to the gunnel, expecting the boat to hurtle forward, she looked at Keoni's broad back, a tattoo of crossed kāhilis on the base of his neck, and said, "Eh Keoni, long time no see. What? They let you out?"

"Nah nah," he said, turning from the wheel, "I wen' escape." He turned the wheel and eased the boat forward, looking once down at the remaining paddler.

Deb number three was sitting on a blue cushion doubled over with her arms around herself. "Are you all right?" Danielle asked.

She shook her head no.

"Got sick early," Kimo said. He draped a large beach towel over Danielle's shoulders and then put his arms around her, his chest against her back. "You cold," he said. "You must get warmed up. An' drink water."

"Thanks." She shivered against him. "Is there any way we can get her off the boat?" Kimo let go of her and went into the cabin, then turned.

"No, everybody occupied. The others trying to keep stuffs together. Radio says the race goes still yet. We'll see."

"We saw three hulis."

"We saw like five or six. The worst may be over."

"There's nothing worse than being sick and having to stay on a boat," she said. She realized that the outsides of her knees were bruised and chafed, from bracing them against the inside of the hull. On the floor of the boat was a cooler tied in place, and she reached down and opened it and got a bottle of water, and drank.

"I asked her," Kimo said. "She says jus' keep going. She'll try to get better."

She turned and saw Michelle shivering under her towel. "You know," she said, "you're damned good. The changes were regular as heartbeats."

"Thanks." Then she laughed. "I can count."

"I tried sitting three once and calling changes," Danielle said. "And you know what? I couldn't count." She leaned away from the gunnel. Judy Beeman was up at the side of the cabin, hanging on and looking ahead.

Once she was able to look around, she realized that Moloka'i, behind them, was barely visible, a hazy flat shape against the flat gray sky, showers maybe, and ahead, she saw nothing. The vague fear caused by seeing nothing ahead caused a little flash of an inward-turning musing, and she put her hand up to her neck and felt the gold chain, and the little loop of hair suspended at the bottom. She sat down and drank water, and stared at the wet deck between her feet, then up at the sick girl, then at the wet deck between her feet. After a while she began to feel anxious to get back in the water, and anxious about not seeing anything of O'ahu.

She got up and edged along the gunnel, the boat rocking up and down in the swells, and said to Kimo, "Where are we?"

He turned, with a conspiratorial expression on his face, looked once at Keoni, and said softly, "Hawai'i."

Okay, so they knew where they were going. A hundred feet ahead the *Keikiali'i* labored over the swells, paddles flashing and every second a hand shooting up with the Clorox bottle bailer throwing out an arc of water. One of the other paddlers wasn't paddling, though—she was aiming for the water and then stopping, the front one. "Hey," she said to Kimo, "something's up with Chrissy. Can we pull up?"

Keoni gunned the engine and moved to the right of the canoe. While he did this, Danielle looked to the left and saw two canoes about a hundred-fifty yards away, one a canoe length ahead of the other, one vanishing under the swells and then the other vanishing, then nosing back up into view. One of them appeared to be koa. Now, from the side, she could see Chrissy Moore looking back and talking, then rolling her shoulders, her paddle across her chest. The others continued to fight the swells, the canoe nosing up and then down, then being pushed sideways by the backwash that ran diagonal to the hull. Tricia worked the paddle, pulling sideways to keep the canoe level. When Chrissy Moore saw the escort boat she pointed at her shoulder.

"I'll go back," Danielle said. She wanted to go back. She wasn't tired, and having to get out of the canoe had felt almost like having something taken from her. "Pull ahead and tell her."

Keoni gunned the motor and moved the boat over the swells, pulling ahead of the canoe by a hundred-fifty feet. Kimo called toward the canoe, and Danielle couldn't understand what he was saying, the clarity of the words stolen by the wind and the sounds of the ocean. Then Kimo turned. "You're on, babes," he said.

She went over the side. The water was cold this time, and treading, waiting for the canoe, she went up and then down so that she couldn't see it, and then up again, and it was twenty feet away and coming, Chrissy Moore rolling off into the water. When the dark hull came at her she positioned herself and then grabbed the gunnel and pulled herself up, scraping across her ribs, and then banging the inside of her knee. When she was in she put her feet down into five inches of water and grabbed the paddle. She looked back once—Donna was bailing.

Again she paddled with that sensation of being a synchronized machine, levers and joints and muscles repeating their smooth motions. Ahead the manu of the *Keikiali'i* rose up and went down across the gray line of the horizon. She still could not see any land, but did see, off to the left now, out in front by a hundred-fifty yards or more, the two canoes she had seen before, one blocking the other so that they rose and settled in the swells, looking oddly like the two blades of clumsily operated scissors. Hut hut ho! and she was pulling on the other side. She had no idea where they were in relation to other canoes. The last? Or maybe in the last quarter. There was no way of knowing and it made no difference. She felt that she could do this all the way, but for one thing: there was a blister forming, she thought, just off the base of the fingers of her right hand, but she ignored it, as she ignored the chafing of the wood against the outsides of her knees and the dull pain throbbing inside her left buttock.

Keoni took the boat out ahead a little, and to the right, and then settled back a little in the swells until they were abreast of the canoe. Kimo leaned out over the gunnel. "Get rain ahead!" he called. "Can see canoes lef' an' escort boats! Stay lef' a little Tricia 'kay?"

Far off was a peculiar picture of a flat gray plane on the right and fat columns of rain on the left coming down from dark-bottomed clouds, the picture divided just above the manu by a wide shaft of white sunlight that caused a path of white on the water the manu ate up. But as she looked, she saw whitecaps out there, as if some rapid change in the wind had come, and she felt it, the southeast wind strengthening so that she could feel it pulling when she raised her paddle for the next stroke. Then, before she thought she should, she felt raindrops stinging her left shoulder, and could see it angling from left down to right, the opposite of what it usually did. Kona weather. They changed over, and paddling on the left side now, she looked ahead at the whitecaps, and the canoe slapped into waves and then heaved up, rested down again. "Rough water!" Kimo called. The sky which had previously been divided by the clouds and the flat gray with the shaft of sun in between was now gone, replaced by a gray as distinct as a painted wall. "Lef' a little," Kimo called, and she felt the canoe slow as Tricia worked her paddle to turn the canoe a little, but carefully, keeping the ama in the water.

They paddled this way, through a light, stinging rain, directed by Kimo who was taking information from Keoni who had the compass. No problem. They'd make their way out of it.

Kimo signaled a change. Judy Beeman would relieve Danielle, Michelle would relieve Marcia. Keoni pulled the boat out ahead, and the two bodies went into the water. Danielle aimed at them, and when they were close, she felt Marcia go off and tried to pull the spray skirt zipper tag forward a little, but it jammed four inches out. She pulled at it, twisting, and it came free. Then she rolled off, the water warm on her skin. "Watch the zipper!" she shouted at Judy. "It gets stuck partway out."

Back on the escort, she pulled herself over to Kimo. "How long've we been going?"

He looked at his watch. "Hour half," he said.

It seemed impossible to her. She had been sure that they were way past the one-third point. She turned and looked out at the *Keikiali'i* rising and nosing down in the swells, the girls paddling at a good pace, set by Judy Beeman, on her way, Danielle thought, to face the music. Marcia was on the other side of the boat talking to the sick Deb, and Chrissy Moore was hanging on the tarp pipe, trying to loosen up her shoulder. "How's that feel?" Danielle asked her.

"I pulled something the other day carrying rocks. Base of the neck."

"Here, you want me to rub it?"

"Yeah."

She made her way over to Chrissy Moore and put both hands up just inside her shoulders, and kneaded with her thumbs, staring at the gold chain resting on her skin, using Chrissy for support as the boat rose and settled. "More toward the neck," she said. "Shit, I get my chance and I blow it. I should never have tried to carry—"

"No no," Danielle said. "You couldn't have known."

The rest Danielle got was not exactly cut short, but she did go back in before she thought she would. Judy Beeman signaled a change. Marcia got herself ready, and this time it would be Donna and Judy. Danielle waited as the canoe approached, and knew why it was that Judy had signaled—she leaned over the hull and threw up liquid into the water. Danielle and Marcia went to the gunnel. "Judy might be out of it," Marcia said.

"All right, that leaves seven of us. We might be almost halfway there."

She laughed. "We might be heading for Palmyra."

They jumped in the water.

As Donna and Judy rolled off and Marcia and Danielle pulled themselves in, Donna shouted, "Kick ass!" Danielle got the skirt zipped to her belly, and again felt her feet planted in five inches of water, which, when the nose of the *Keikiali'i* rose, sloshed away. The escort boat drifted to the right, sixty feet away, Keoni hunched over the wheel. Then Kimo was leaning out again. "More rain ahead!" he called. "Bettah conditions odda side!"

Paddling, she imagined that they were heading toward a curtain, beyond which might be sunlight. The curtain was a thick column of rain, miles wide, angling down to the right, and in the middle distance she caught a brief glimpse of canoes and escort boats, far to their left. The blister on her right hand began to bother her, and she tried to ignore it, as she tried to ignore the growing stabs of pain in her stomach and lower back, and in her shoulder joints. The numbness in her buttocks had gone away and been replaced by a tenderness she associated with being bruised, and skin had opened up a little on the outsides of her knees.

But the rhythm of paddling pushed the pain into the back of her mind, and she responded to the change calls automatically, keeping her eye on the upward projection of the *Keikiali'i*'s manu, which remained there solidly in place, seemingly separate from the dancing ocean and the thin, angled lines of rain ahead, the entire plane of ocean and gray sky divided horizontally tipping up and back, sliding high into her vision and then low under the manu. And then they entered the rain and behind her there was a scream, then a whoop of exhilaration. It pelted her scalp, stung her shoulders and knees, and ran down her forehead and upper lip, so that with each breath she blew droplets of it away from her mouth. And then as the rain intensified, the water ahead seemed to boil with steam, and the hissing sound of it hitting the water made the change call sound flat and distant, even though it came from five or six feet behind her. It caused a strange lapse for her, as if in a slow, dizzying flash she had paddled her way into a bizarre dream, soundless and hollow, and ahead off to her right, shapes materialized on the water, ghostly, translucent canoes knifing through, oblivious of the swells, and then they seemed to sharpen so that she saw that they were paddled by dark, hunched over men, and she thought they must be war canoes, and she felt herself knifing with them, weightless and powerful, laughing inside, the dizzy and exhilarating expenditure of energy painless and forceful and time itself no longer a linear thing but total, as if she were paddling five hundred years ago and also paddling in the present, and paddling in all the times in between with different people behind her, some of them long dead and some of them not even born yet and she was awed by her luck at breaking out of time and seeing something no human had seen as the dark shapes forced their paddles through the water and she forced her paddle through the water and it was as if she were being born all over and remade somehow, ushered into life by war canoes five hundred years old, and she looked for them again to her right, and saw nothing but wind-lashed waves and rain hissing on the water and beyond that, the dim shape of Keoni's boat nosing up and then down, exhaust smoke sitting briefly on the water before dispersing into the wind. When the change call came to her, again flat against the hissing of rain on the water, she changed into her stinging right hand and wondered how long that strange vision had taken, whether five seconds or twenty minutes, and could not remember.

The swells increased, so that like before the canoe began clearing water so high that she couldn't get anything with her paddle. And then the nose would slam down, water sloshing over the pale kai and the skirt. The water on her feet had risen, and behind she could feel the movement of someone bailing. Tricia kept riding the swells down to the right, and then turning the canoe back when they passed.

Settling further into the rhythm of paddling, she again felt pulled in, the hissing of the rain on the water shutting out full awareness of where she was or what was happening. The reassuring sound of the gunning of Keoni's engine came across the water, and the change calls came from behind, and she stroked, the canoe being pushed by the swells so that her feet, planted in the water and on the wood, constantly flexed, holding her in place, her knees braced against the inside of the hull. She held to this half-conscious expenditure of force imagining that nothing hurt, and was halfway into sending the paddle into the water when she caught air and the horizon tipped to vertical and her face slapped the water and she was inverted in the water, the paddle gone and sound shut out, and she twisted sideways to reach for the paddle. She felt around for it, her hands moving in the warm, heavy medium, and then she curled herself inward, water stinging the inside of her nose and her eyes, which stared with a confused awe at the fuzzy movement of her hands and her hair waving snakelike before her eyes, and she fumbled down at her waist for the skirt zipper. She was supposed to simply slide out, but wanted that little extra space, so she got the zipper and pulled, but it was jammed, and because she had twisted in her seat reaching for the paddle, she had no purchase on the floor of the hull, and tugged at the zipper tongue, and it gave a little and then stopped, and then she put both hands on the canvas and pulled, but the zipper was too tight. She felt halting convulsions in her throat, and again addressed the zipper tongue and pulled, hurting her fingers. She gripped the hull and pulled herself up, but with her legs sideways she couldn't get her feet on anything. For one moment the confusion robbed her of any will, and she felt her chest heaving inward with a painful, involuntary force. She turned herself back into an upside down sitting position and planted her feet on the floor and pushed as if rising, as if trying to lift something incredibly heavy, the tarp stretched tight across her thighs, and the tarp burst free, the zipper scraping across her thighs, and she swam out to the right and surfaced coughing and then gasping, the rain stinging her face, and saw her paddle dancing ten feet away on a swell and swam after it. When she reached the paddle and turned back to the canoe she saw that it wasn't there—the water steamed with the rain pelting it, and all around her was a flat gray, the pelted water sending up clouds of what looked like steam, and she rotated and saw nothing, only the fuzzy surface of the ocean and the rain pelting it and that dense steam rising so that there was no longer any division between water and sky, and she reached up to pull hair from her eyes and felt her neck and found that the chain was not there—it was gone, the chain and the loop of hair, and that caused a flash of horrible fright to race through her, and she held onto the paddle and then heard sharp voices, people yelling her name, and when she heard the voices she saw the faint, spectral shape of the ama rising up and falling and the faint sound of it slapping down, then the shape of the canoe, and swam toward it. "I lost my—" They were bailing with the Clorox bottles and with their hands. When she got to the canoe she reached in and pulled water out with her hands, heard Tricia yelling but could not understand what she was saying and she kept on pulling water from the hull, out from the hole in the tarp, and the sound of Keoni's boat was close now, the garbled sound of talking—you guys okay? Danny, you okay?—and she pulled water from the hull, the level inching down now, and the canoe rose in a swell and then settled, and then they began to climb in while bailing, she too, banging her hip and scraping her ribs as she went, and once in the seat, she reached down below her knees and threw more water out over the V-shaped rip in the tarp, and heard them talking in sharp, dreamlike sentences she couldn't understand, and then she felt the canoe begin to move, and set her paddle and stroked.

Three of them paddled and three bailed, one with her hands. Then four of them paddled and two of them bailed. Then five of them paddled and one of them bailed. And then all of them paddled. The *Keikiali'i* rose and settled, was twisted from its course by swells and was steered back, and after a few minutes they found they were forty yards behind two canoes, one of them dark, and she saw it list sideways in a swell. Koa.

"Steady!" Tricia yelled. "Hold the pace!" Danielle laughed and tried to set a pace, and settled back into the rhythm, the manu of the *Keikiali'i* again seeming nailed to a spot under the horizon, sweeping up and over those two canoes in the swells. The rain was letting up. Keoni's boat moved out ahead, sixty feet to their right, and then slowed down so that they were abreast of it, and Kimo called out, "Stay right—pass um onna right Tricia. Bettah ahead."

Bettah ahead. Then she thought, pass them? The directive seemed foolish, coming from an optimism that wasn't warranted, but Danielle picked up the pace, again aware of the pain in her hand and the stinging of water on the outsides of her knees and the dull, burning ache of all her muscles and the bruises and chafes. But as they paddled, she was aware that the canoes, now ahead to the left, were getting closer, and the swells were not as large, and ahead the sky was not as gray, and the manu stayed in its spot, going toward what now appeared to be a brightening strip across the horizon. Then, after a period of time she could not calculate because she stopped thinking and responded only to the change calls, that strip thickened and became a blinding silver, all the way across, the two canoes out to their left breaking into it and vanishing in a flashing silver and then reappearing, one against the other, the closer one the koa, the dark shapes of the paddlers above the shape of the canoe moving in a dreamlike rhythm with its paddles and elbows and bodies, and making that part of the blinding strip of silver pulse and flash, and then from behind her she heard a whoop, and then another, and she didn't know why until she looked up to her right and there, through the remaining rain, faint but huge above the blinding silver strip, sat the broad shape of Oʻahu, a mass you could see and not see at the same time, and when she looked again she saw it sitting solidly on the silver strip while the canoe danced in the swells, a shifting translucent mass, much bigger than she thought it should be, now faint shapes visible against the mass, brighter spots, color even, buildings, the darker areas of trees in the mountains, and the dark profile on top rising into white clouds.

Then the two canoes ahead to their left brightened and took on color, the shirts of the paddlers green where they were gray before, and within a couple of minutes she saw the deepening color of her own forearms, and the ocean became blue, and she began to feel warmth on her skin.

"Tricia!" Kimo called. "See ahead right—dat big mountain—'ass Makapuʻu Point. Look lef' you see da rounded mountain coming out lef'—'ass Koko Head. Da nex' one sticking out is Portlock. Head for Portlock. We smoke their asses with the inside line 'kay? We go right pass the rocks—you be able to touch um 'kay?"

The inside line. Danielle could tell now that Tricia had adjusted the direction, and the manu had nailed itself to that spot, Portlock, the projection of the manu moving down, then up, like someone slowly pointing, over and over, at Portlock. The two canoes ahead of them were farther left now, but not really angling away it seemed. "Time for a change!" Kimo called. "Who like rest?"

"Marcia!" Danielle called over her shoulder. "Take a break!"

Keoni drew the boat out ahead a hundred yards, and then it turned a little. They paddled toward it, and Oʻahu had clarified, now seeming immense and rich in color, and Danielle scanned the horizon as they approached the boat and way out ahead saw more canoes—yellow, blue, and escort boats, and could not believe that the *Keikialiʻi* had kept with them, and she saw Keoni move the boat so as not to impede their forward movement, and then Donna went off

119

the side and swam into position, and when she felt Marcia go off the side she turned quickly to look and saw, behind them, a canoe and its escort boat, and again thought that something had to be wrong, that their position was too good. Then, when she felt Donna getting in, felt thumping on the hull, and then felt the canoe rise a little, as if Donna had dug her paddle with all the force she had, Danielle dug her paddle too, increasing the pace a little, and was about to yell when Tricia did it for her: "Dig! Kick ass! Eat um up!"

Her hand began to bleed a little—she saw it staining the paddle-handle. Aimed as they were for Portlock, it seemed that the koa ahead of them and to the left, twice as far ahead as they were before, had taken some kind of bait and turned to parallel them, and that seemed to draw the third canoe, out farther ahead, in the same direction. But that perception was wrong. They knew where they were going, and it was as if the *Keikiali'i* were following them. Far ahead other escort boats bobbed in the waves, their canoes not visible, six or seven hundred yards out.

Keoni had apparently watched the other koa, because when its escort boat moved out in front, it meant a change, and so he pulled closer. "Danny!" Kimo called. "Marcia stroke for you!"

"No!"

"Ten minutes—you go back! Garans!"

She kept paddling.

"Do it," Michelle called to her. "Because you gotta take us in."

Marcia was in the water, and as the canoe approached her, Danielle rolled off and moved off to the side, and Marcia grabbed the gunnel and struggled up inside. The canoe left, and Keoni pulled the boat to her. She made her way into the boat, to find Judy and the other girl sitting next to each other doubled over, while Chrissy Moore was up next to Keoni. She turned, held up her left arm with her right hand, and shook her head. Kimo came back with a towel. She wrapped it around herself. "Drink water," he said. "Bloat yourself. Nex' time you change, you gotta stay. Chrissy can't move her shoulder. Marcia's outta gas."

"Where are we?"

"No mo' pleasure cruise babe. We're in it. Shitload behind us."

"My hand's hurt."

She held it up and he looked at it. "Wait—get tape." He fumbled in the little first-aid kit, then stood up and said something to Keoni, who shrugged and continued looking ahead. Then Kimo found his tee shirt, put it down on the deck, stepped on one of the short sleeves and pulled up, ripping the sleeve off. He came back with a roll of tape and the piece of shirt. "'Kay," he said, and began wrapping the palm of her hand. When he had the shirtsleeve tight, he said, "Grab this bar 'kay?"

She did so, and it seemed to work.

"'Kay," he said, and taped the shirtsleeve in place.

"I wanna go back now."

"Cool yoa jets 'kay? Still a long way." He looked closely at her face. "Where you was when the canoe hulied?"

"Upside down in the canoe."

"I was like ready to go in."

"No, I was all right. The zipper got stuck. I know I was just supposed to wriggle out, but I got turned so I couldn't get out right away. I was more confused than anything else, I think."

She made her way to Judy and, holding onto the tarp pipe and standing above her, said, "How you guys feel?"

Judy looked up. "We're all right as long as we don't move." She laughed. "What'd I tell you?"

"Hey, you made it more than halfway."

She nodded. "Next year," she said. "Well, maybe. If I can get past this stuff."

"You'll make it."

The Deb, whose name Danielle now remembered as Lauren something, looked up, pale and tired.

"Sorry about that," she said. "This doesn't usually happen."

"Hey, without you we wouldn't have even been allowed to go."

Danielle looked back. She counted the escort boats she could see behind them—six, no, seven, and spots behind them that may or may not have been escort boats. Ahead, the two canoes they were tracking seemed to have extended their lead, and that made her want to get back in the canoe.

When she was back in the canoe, for the rest of the way, she had Michelle behind her, who had been relieved by Marcia for ten minutes, and then behind Michelle sat Nikki, then Donna and Kathy Shimabukuro and finally, Tricia, who was staying in her seat, black-and-blue 'okole or not. Marcia would relieve anyone who wanted relief somewhere around Portlock, and then someone else when they made it across Maunalua Bay. The koa canoe they had been tailing remained seventy-five to a hundred yards ahead of them, and as she paddled, her eyes locked on the manu of the *Keikiali'i*, she watched the rhythmic collective movement of their paddles, and watched the looming red and brown shape of Portlock enlarge. Marcia relieved Kathy Shimabukuro. The koa ahead of them was also taking an inside line, so if they were going to overtake it, they were going to have to paddle past it on the outside. And as they approached the high rocks, she saw people standing on them in different colored tee shirts, some with cameras in their hands. Then, closer yet, something happened to sound—it seemed to echo off the rocks they approached, so that everything she heard, she heard as if with some kind of improved hearing, water and bodies moving and breath and the slapping of the prow on the waves somehow rich and precise. And as Kimo had told them would happen, they paddled right under the rocks, the water sloshing up against them in white sprays that shot back out at them, the roar of sound so tangible that she lost her concentration. They were no more than forty feet from the rocks, and she heard whoops, whistles, garbled calling, and kept on paddling, until they were past Portlock and broke out into open ocean again, crossing Maunalua Bay, just a hundred yards outside of curling waves that started as long, rounded lumps in the water, which rose, changed color to a lighter blue, and then dropped, followed by upward blasts of spray and occasionally, a surfboard soaring and then falling. Beyond the waves, she briefly caught the glint of traffic moving on Kalaniana'ole Highway, crossing behind a couple of white mast poles in the bay.

Keoni kept the boat on the inside of them, to assess the beginnings of sets to make sure they weren't getting too close. Again Keoni's boat went up ahead, and Kathy Shimabukuro dropped into the water, and relieved Marcia in a transfer so efficient that the canoe did not seem to lose any speed. The span across Maunalua Bay was almost serene, felt to her almost like practice, where she waited for the change call, went over and continued, and the only thing that impeded a total engagement in the process of moving muscles and the pinioning of joints was the wound on the top of the palm of her hand, which had now stained Kimo's shirtsleeve a faint pink.

The next marker she recognized, looming before the oddly shaped profile of Diamond Head from the back side, was Black Point, dark with greenery and large houses. From the perspective of flatter water she quickly scanned the horizon as she paddled, and saw a barge, saw shapes of escort boats, and a hundred yards ahead, the same koa canoe. It had maintained its lead across the bay, and was now entering somewhat rougher water as it moved in closer to Black Point.

Following a tentative sensation of a kind of competitive willfulness creep into her, she very slightly increased the pace, and felt that slight increase in the muscular force necessary to maintain that pace. "Right," Michelle said. "Now's the time. That's right, just pick it up a little." And then, when her paddle swept back through the water, she increased the force she pulled with, felt it in her shoulders, lower back, and in her feet planted on the hull floor. Her grip on the paddle handle tightened, and she eyed the koa canoe ahead and then slightly increased the pace again, and increased the exertion of force she was using to pull the paddle past the hull. She kept her breathing synchronized with the stroking, and tried holding this pace for two changes, and hearing nothing in the way of protest from behind her, held that pace until the koa ahead of them seemed a little closer. "'Ass it!" Kimo called. "Plenny time—you narrowed um. No back off 'kay? Tricia, cut left a little 'kay?"

She felt the slight movement, but did not alter the pace or the force of the strokes. The koa ahead of them had also turned a little so that again, the shiny brown projection of the *Keikiali'i*'s manu actually touched that other koa when little swells lifted the front of the canoe. Keoni pulled the boat ahead a little, and she caught sight of Marcia leaning out over the gunnel. "Eh, you teenagers!" she called. "I pau areddy! I all shaky an' kapakahi! My 'ōpū get cramps! Las' chance fo' change. But I tell you, I only slow you down!"

"Who's tired?" Tricia shouted.

"We're okay!" Nikki shouted. "We take it in!"

"Kimo says cut lef' Tricia!" Marcia shouted. "You listing in too far! He says, what, you like beach um Kāhala?"

The canoe turned a little, putting the manu on the koa ahead of them.

"Kick it!" Marcia called. "Pass um and give stink-eye when you do!"

The escort boat for the koa ahead of them moved out ahead of the koa. "They'll change before Diamond Head!" Donna called. "They're gonna change now!"

Danielle concentrated on her stroke, and then increased the pace again, and increased the force of the paddle pulling past the hull. "Little more," Michelle called to her, so she increased the pace and the force a little more, concentrating on the stroke, this time looking down, her eyes on the water sweeping past, and her feet remained planted on the floor of the hull, her breathing kept with the stroke. She did not look up to see what the other canoe was doing. She kept at this until she saw ahead the heavier water, and the canoe shifted its direction—they were going outside the other koa. She saw the escort close to it now, and caught a brief glimpse of figures in the water.

They moved abreast of the other koa canoe just as they entered the swells off Diamond Head. She kept her stroke, aware that the swells were not as high as those at the beginning, and when the call came to stroke on the right side, she saw the huge projection of the parched, rocky flank of Diamond Head, and the sweep of sailboards outside the break, and for a second, the kiawe spotted hillside just up from the beach and below the line defining the wall of the parking spaces on Diamond Head Road, and she thought of Herman Prince and Peggy MacNeil, sitting close together in this canoe somewhere along that beach a half a century ago, Herman Prince pointing at a flower above her ear and asking her where she found it, and when the change call came for her to stroke on the left, she thought that surely there should have been something in Peggy MacNeil's life to rescue her from that rope. Halfway across the break she began to see the hotel buildings in the distance, and she thought that even a sympathetic neighbor, or a canoe with potted orchids on it, blooming in the back of a metal-roofed shed, could almost have been enough. And when she looked briefly to her side and saw the other koa canoe abreast of them thirty-five yards away or so, she increased the pace and increased the force necessary to maintain that pace, and thought that all she could do was pity Peggy MacNeil, not so much because of the tragedy in her life, but because of her youthful failure to simply be patient enough to keep looking for something, anything to rescue her from that rope.

Waikīkī. When the bright expanse of buildings opened up to their right, she heard whoops behind her, and kept the pace, the koa to their right exactly abreast of them, seemingly mirrored, even in the strokes. She was aware now that there were escort boats and other canoes out from them, and ahead of them, and briefly eyed the buildings, setting them in her mind so that she could see the end above the *Keikialiʻi*'s manu, the distant spot of an orange buoy, and a cluster of escort boats outside Fort DeRussy Beach, where it would end.

The koa abreast of them was preparing for another change, the last one, most likely, and the *Keikialiʻi*'s last chance to get a lead on them. They were making the change closer in toward the beginnings of the sets than they should, it seemed, and apparently Keoni picked up on this too, because he called out, "Tricia, cut left, an' when they roll off, kick it on the outside 'kay? Too sloppy inside so cut left an' kick ass!"

Danielle felt the canoe turn a little, and kept her eyes on the figures on the escort boat for the other canoe. They were doing it perfectly—the three dropping from the escort boat and then lining up. She held her pace, waiting, and then, when the figures in the canoe rolled off into the water, she pulled hard until she was paddling at a near sprint, and the rest picked up on it too, because, as she peeked to the side, she saw the shape of the koa in her peripheral vision slide back, and caught just a glimpse of figures struggling to get on the canoe. She held onto the pace, stroking with as much force as the burning pain would allow, and concentrated on keeping the strokes smooth, as if carefully practicing what a coach was telling her—no lunging, pull the water past, a fluid move. Rhythm, balance, and power.

The large orange buoy was there, and sat there, seemingly at a fixed distance as she paddled. She knew they were narrowing the distance to it, but it felt as if the ball were also shrinking in size as they approached, or they were simply not moving. Her breathing now stung her throat, and her arms felt so weary that they felt as if they might drop involuntarily, but she held to the stroke, and behind her everyone else held to theirs. She lapsed into such full concentration on the stroking, eyes locked on the ball ahead which rose and dropped in relation to the manu of the *Keikialiʻi*, that she did not hear something Kimo yelled, and dully realized that those sounds came from the ocean side of the canoe rather than the beach side. It took her ten seconds of stroking, gasping for breath, and trying to hold her arms up, to realize that he had moved the escort outside to allow the canoe to go on by itself into the chute. Their job was done.

Then she was aware, stroking on the right side, that the other koa had come nearly abreast of them again, and tried to increase the pace, but there seemed to be nothing left in her arms, and her entire upper body felt as if it wanted to curl in on itself. The shape continued to move up, the arms and paddles at a pace exceeding theirs, and as the buoy approached, suddenly huge now that she looked up at it again, she was aware that the other koa's inside line gave the lead over to them, and although she tried to increase the pace, to sprint past them, she felt Tricia nudge the canoe to give the other one the path into the chute.

She had been barely aware, she realized, of the garbled blatting from a loudspeaker system, and when she felt the sharp turn to the right, the manu of the *Keikialiʻi* sweeping across a blur of bright colors on the beach, she heard chanting over the sound of the loudspeakers, men chanting in Hawaiian as the two canoes swept along the pilings of the jetty topped by the tent, and she thought at first that the chanting was because one canoe had beaten the other. But that wasn't it. The chanting, she realized, still pulling toward the finish line, was for both canoes, because they were the wood of war canoes, the flesh and blood and bones of voyaging canoes. And when they crossed the finish line, she took one moment to hold the paddle over her head before her arms became too weak and her body curled in on itself with a heavy, cramping pain, from her knees all the way to her neck. She felt a hand on her back, heard the dreamlike chattering of voices, and tried to resist the urge to vomit. The urge went away, and she tried sitting up, her hands trembling, her neck weak, and looked at the sodden, pink wrapping around her right hand, one line of blood coming five inches up her wrist. Pink seawater dripped out of Kimo's shirtsleeve into the hull. She stared at the line of blood on her wrist, now dispersing a little over the skin, and it locked her into a haunted fascination, and her mind went into a strange, soundless dream that felt to her like suddenly finding herself in the middle of space somewhere, a long dizzying sweep as if she were emerging from a dream, floating painlessly amid planets and stars, absolutely alone but then not alone, and it made her laugh—vaguely she thought that she was fainting or had become deaf, but when she looked out over the manu, she saw the bright colors on the beach and heard the sounds of voices, and the lines of people, many of them with leis hanging from their wrists and cameras to their faces.

She slid her paddle into the front of the canoe and rolled off into the water, and now that it was done every ding on her knees, and the wound on her hand, stung. She ran her right hand in the water and then lifted it and squeezed the water out of the shirtsleeve. She heard coughing behind her, then groans and talk. Donna was there next to her, her arm over her shoulder. "That was great," she said. "Man, that was great."

"Yeah." The others were up at the front of the canoe now, arms around her, and she kept saying, "Yeah, it was. Yeah, yeah."

"Is that your dad up there?" Donna asked.

She looked. He was coming into the water in his shorts, and wore one of the souvenir tee shirts. He was carrying a lei.

"Hey Dad," she said.

"I almost missed you," he said. "You guys must be good." He put the lei over her head. Cigar flower. It scratched her neck a little, and she shuddered. He put his arms around her.

"Watch your shirt."

"Nah. Forget the shirt. When you're ready, come on over to DeRussy Park. We staked out a table. Got food and stuff."

"Thanks." She looked at him. His expression was a combination of concern and joviality.

"You did well. How are you?"

"I'm fine," she said. "Dinged up but fine."

Donna waded over to them and said, "Mr. Baker, hello."

"Oh, this is Donna," Danielle said. They shook hands.

"Sorry to interrupt," Donna said, "but they say we've gotta take the canoe away now, over to the Hilton Lagoon area."

The others were climbing back in. "Okay," Danielle said

"What's that on your hand?" he asked.

"A sleeve from Kimo's shirt. I got a blister. It's okay." Her hands shaky, she peeled off the gauze tape, pulled the pink, soggy shirtsleeve off, and looked at the palm of her hand.

"Yeah," he said, "it's separated a little, with like a cut. They've got a tent over there with stuff for that."

"Okay," she said. She closed her hand into a fist because it felt better that way.

"So this is it," he said, wading past her a little. "Good looking canoe."

"Yeah, did Kimo tell you about it?" She walked along the hull and worked her way back into her seat.

"Yeah. Said it had no cracks. I guess because you brought it over I should ask you what we should do with it."

"I don't know," she said. "Did he say whose it was?"

Her father looked at her. He shrugged, and said, "No, just that it was in the shed and that it was old. I assumed it was junk."

129

"Look, I want to talk to you about the canoe. I mean, I want to make a deal, because I want to keep it."

"Well, sure, we can—"

"Hui!" Donna called. Danielle turned and nodded.

"Seriously, how do you feel?" her father asked.

"I'm fine. I feel all right." She pulled her paddle out of the hull.

He didn't appear convinced. The look of skepticism on his face turned to a look of a kind of good-humored suspicion. "All right all right? Or just all right?"

"I'm fine," she said. "I'll get this taken care of, and meet you up at the table. Where is it?"

"Back side. Just walk through all the people."

She showered holding her hand out in the air, the lei in it, so that the new bandage and the lei would not get wet. Other girls showering seemed so much more happy and energetic than she felt that she wondered if something was wrong with her. One of them asked her if she was on that koa number sixty-whatever and she said yes, and the girl told her that she had been in the canoe that was just ahead of them. "You pushed us in," she said. And Danielle said, "Thanks, because you pulled us in." Then she put the lei back on and went, still wet, across the grass, past the groups of people singing and the kids and the smells of cooking that made her vaguely nauseated, to the table. Donna and The Debs, The Airheads, Judy, and Marcia were there. Tricia and her Honolulu recruits were not. Then, when she looked at them all, sitting there either on the concrete benches or on the grass near the table, she thought that she should not think of them by their nicknames any more. "Where's Tricia?"

"She and the other girls are at the tent looking at where we came in," Donna said. "People said some of the koas are still out."

"Really?"

"What about Keoni and Kimo?"

"They're taking the boat over to behind the Ilikai—like a slip there they can leave it in for now. The canoe's still on the lagoon beach, and Kimo said Keoni's got a trailer. Your dad's gonna meet them and get a bunch of the guys from Outrigger or something to help them load it."

"Jesus, he thought of everything."

"Sure did. It's gonna be a while before we can eat." Donna looked at the coolers, and at the black hemisphere of a grill sitting along with the paddles in a patch of sunlight a few feet away from the table.

"I don't wanna eat now anyway," Danielle said.

She found a place to sit down, on the end of one of the benches. She put her forearms on the cold concrete table and rested her head on them, the lei hanging between her wrists. "I'll just sleep for a while," she said.

"I've been thinking," Donna said. She was sitting next to Danielle and had moved close to her, and the statement came almost as a whisper.

"I haven't," Danielle said.

"No, I'm serious."

"Okay, shoot."

"Can you do computer stuff?"

"Most of it, yeah."

"Power Point? Excel? Spreadsheets?"

"Yeah, I could figure that out. Why?"

Donna didn't speak. Danielle raised her head from her arms to look at her, and she was staring off toward the ocean, her eyebrows down.

"Why?"

131

"You know," Donna said, "I'm really tired of sitting around and feeling like shit about last year. I'm really tired of it."

"Good for you. I mean it."

She saw Tricia coming their way, walking around blankets, kind of fast, it seemed. When she got to the table, she folded her arms across her chest and frowned, as if she wasn't sure of what she wanted to say. "Okay," she said. "You're not going to believe this. We came in third in the koa division. A couple of koas had trouble in the rough water. One had to be towed because their rigging had trouble, you know, broken cords or something. So we came in third. I think we're getting a trophy."

"I don't believe that," Danielle said, and put her head back down on her arms, and looked at the loop of the lei hanging there. The other girls were up, asking her if she was sure, did she really see the name *Keikialiʻi* or the number, or whatever, on the list? Yes, she had. Third, and there was no question about it. Some of them were still out. Judy and Marcia got up and headed toward the tent, as if they did not believe what Tricia had said.

"So anyway," Donna said.

"Anyway?"

"About computers and all that. About being tired of being a wimp. I've been on the phone with a couple of people, just in the past few days. I've got a chance to open an office here, do a tax service. This old man I know is retiring and going out of business, and he still has some accounts that he does. He said he'd give those accounts to me. Do you do your own taxes?"

"No, I have mine done by the blockheads."

"This would be up in Kaimukī, good rental situation, a nice office—I mean I've seen it, and Kaimukī's become a pretty little town, you know, coffee shops and stuff like that. How'd you like to go into business as a tax preparer?"

"It sounds—" She laughed. Donna laughed too.

"I know. The excitement would be overwhelming."

"But I think I could handle," Danielle said. "Yeah, I could. Gainful employment. What would you pay me?"

"Minimum, at first. I'm not like a tax mogul yet. By and by you'd get blockhead salary. Garans, as your brother says."

"F'real?"

"Yup. What do you think?"

"Could I go home weekends?"

"Of course. What do you mean 'home'?"

"I mean Moloka'i," she said. She raised her head off her arms and looked around, and adjusted the lei so that it didn't irritate the back of her neck. She felt a little better, and the nausea had gone away. Donna was squinting at her skeptically, a look almost too much like the look her father had given her.

"I thought you said you felt banished there."

"No. I like it."

"I do, too. I guess I'd go home weekends too. But if you're interested, we can try to get it going right away. Right now the old dude goes in two days a week and sits there and looks out the window. We can spend some time with him and get a feel for the business." She laughed. "How's this? I'm thinking that I'd like to meet some nice man. I mean, the company of women is great and all, but you know—" She didn't continue.

"What?"

"I just think I'm sort of ready for that now."

"I'm not," Danielle said. "Maybe after I do somebody's taxes, then I'll be ready."

"Do the E-Z form then."

Danielle laughed. "That's cheating."

Tricia was now sitting across from them, on the middle of the bench. Behind her on the grass, together, were The Debs, and Danielle concentrated: Nikki, Kathy, and Lauren. She wanted to make sure she wouldn't forget them.

Now Tricia was looking at Donna and Danielle, her expression odd, as if she wanted to say something but thought better of it.

"What?" Danielle said.

She took a deep breath, and then looked away.

"Tricia," Danielle said, "you're being mysterious again."

"I wanted to—" She looked around. "I wanted to wait until Judy and Marcia could be here." And she looked at Chrissy Moore and Michelle Forten. "And them too."

"For what?"

Her eyes dropped to Danielle's neck. "What happened to your chain?"

"It fell off out there. Broke or something, when we hulied, I think."

"I can make another. I have a couple more loops of hair. Or you might inherit Judy's."

"I'd like to have another one."

Danielle saw Marcia and Judy making their way around the groups of people and the beach mats and quilts. Marcia nodded enthusiastically from fifty feet. So it was true. Judy, on the other hand, walked looking around her like a tourist visiting this place for the first time.

When they arrived, Tricia got up from the bench and went over to talk to them, and then to Michelle and Chrissy. Then the five of them came back, and sat at the table, crowded on the concrete benches. Tricia went and talked briefly to her three friends on the grass, and they waved their hands, one saying, "No problem. We don't want to move anyway." Tricia came back, sat down, and took another deep breath. "'Kay," she said. "I want to invite you guys to a reading." She paused, and then got a sort of mortified look, as if she were shocked at what she had just said. "Well, 'kay, it's me doing the reading."

"When is this?" Donna asked.

"Tuesday, day after tomorrow, at the University. Actually it's three people reading, myself and two graduate students."

"Didn't you say you could never do that?" Donna asked.

"I did, and I can't. I'm scared."

"What are you reading?" Judy asked.

"'Kay, it's that I started writing the story. I mean about Herman Prince and Peggy MacNeil. I sent this by e-mail to my mentor? You know the lady I told you about, the one who got me writing poetry and stuff? She's like in her sixties, early sixties maybe, sometimes walks with a cane? She's sort of tough and uncompromising, and when she e-mailed me she said it was the best thing I'd ever written and better than this and that. She said that now it's time for me to read. She said what I wrote was good enough to get into print, and she said she was arranging to show part of it to a magazine, and she was arranging a reading for some students and decided to put me in the lineup too, and if I didn't show then it would be my problem, and I'll tell you I'm so scared that I don't think I can do this, I mean, if you aren't there? Could you come?"

"Sure," Danielle said. "I can stay until Tuesday."

"You'll have to stay until even later than that," Donna said. "We've gotta do some work in Kaimukī. And it's not taxes yet. It's like fixing the office up. Mops, buckets, and stuff like that. We slide Mr. Stevens over here, mop a little, then slide him back to the window. Stuff like that."

"You mean I'm already on the payroll?"

"Yeah. Could you run over there and get me a cup of coffee please?"

"I get it."

"I'll come," Judy said. "I'll let you know where I'm staying, even if it is Halawa High Security."

"They wouldn't do that, would they?" Donna asked.

"Probably not. Look," and she sighed once, quickly. "I was only joking. I wish it could be some other way, but I'm bailing out of this. I convinced myself that I'd do it, and now I can't. I'll call my husband and tell him maybe next year. I know. I'm a chicken."

"Well," Danielle said, "you have to be ready for something like that."

"I know, and I'm not." She shook her head, and for a moment looked as if she might cry. "You guys can keep mum about this?"

"Sure," Donna said. Danielle caught the look on Donna's face. It was a combination of disappointment and sympathy. She had come this far, but it wasn't enough.

"I'll come to your reading, though," Judy said, seeming to brighten up a little.

"I cannot stay," Marcia said. "I wish I could, but no can. An' no worry about bagging, Judy. You gotta be ready for that."

"Yeah, I know," Judy said. "But he sounds changed enough that—" She shook her head and looked around. "But I can't yet. I want to go home." The look on her face now seemed bleak and devastated, and again she tried to shake it off. "You guys going to stay?" she asked.

Michelle Forten looked at Chrissy Moore. "It's like," Michelle said. "Well, we hafta go back tonight."

"Aren't you going to stay in Waikīkī?" Donna asked.

"No, we're like going back to some stuff we—" She shook her head. "The Kama brothers are going to take us to a taro patch."

"Or kalo I guess would be the right word," Chrissy said. "Besides, I gotta get back to the hotel, too. Really, I'd love to stay, but there's this stuff we're kind of committed to. The kalo patch thing."

"Yeah, kalo," Michelle said. "Anyway, we're going to work in a kalo patch. Don't ask me how we got into that. We just did, and actually it's a lot of fun, and you learn a lot of stuff. So we're doing that, then we work at the Kaluako'i."

Danielle looked at them. All the jewelry they had on now was the chain with the loop of Peggy MacNeil's hair.

"You guys should go back and do that," she said. "I like what you're doing. I really do."

"You know," Chrissy said, "I don't want to lose contact. I mean, we can set stuff up for next year too, right?"

"Which means you're staying on Molokaʻi?"

"Well," Chrissy said, and then looked at Michelle. "I don't know. Molokaʻi's kind of its own thing, and then—"

She did not continue, so Michelle said, "Well, who knows?"

"We can set stuff up for next year," Danielle said. "We should keep in touch. I'd like that."

"I can still be a part of this too, right?" Judy asked.

"Of course," Marcia said.

No one spoke for five seconds. Danielle caught looks, concealed embarrassment, feigned interest in what was happening near the beach.

"So anyway," Donna said, turning back to Tricia. "What is this thing you wrote called?" The question brought them all back, and Judy appeared relieved.

Tricia took a deep breath, and then thought a moment, looking down at the table. "Well, it's a little more complicated than I led you to believe," she said. "I finished one of the things, a shorter book sort of, the one my mentor is showing to a magazine? Actually she says that only part would be in a magazine. The entire thing would be a book. I don't have a title yet. I've been beating my brains out on that, but I come up empty."

"Do they like, pay you?" Chrissy Moore asked.

"No, it just appears in the magazine."

Chrissy nodded, then looked somewhat skeptically at Michelle.

"That's not all of it," Tricia went on. "The other is a longer book I'm working on about Waikīkī in the forties, with the two characters. The first shorter one is, well, sort of like us. I mean about ourselves."

"Do you write by your own name?" Donna asked.

"I use T. M. Nakamoto."

"Us," Danielle said. "You mean we're in it? You've got Waikīkī in the forties and then something with us?"

"Well, sort of," Tricia said.

"And the one you're reading from is the one we're in?"

"Yeah, that's the more modern one about finding the orchids and the canoe, and the people who take the canoe out and all that."

"Take the canoe out?" Donna said. "Do you mean that the people in your book race the canoe?"

"Yeah, they do."

"You mean like the channel race?"

"Yeah, they do that."

"Where do they come in?"

"Well, I don't know. I changed it a couple times. First would be too, what? Cute, I guess the word would be. So they don't come in first."

Danielle stared at her, waiting for her to say more, but she did not. "Okay," she said, "why were there seven orchids? Why not five or ten?"

"It took me a while to figure that out," Tricia said. "I stayed up a lot at night thinking about it, kinda scared to think about it but thinking anyway, and I decided what it was. I think it was one orchid for each year she waited. Molly said that she committed suicide on the fourth day of nineteen-fifty-five. There was no eighth year, so there was no eighth orchid." She stopped. "Hey," she said.

"Hey what?"

She got this strange look, and then, almost imperceptibly, her mouth moved. She was whispering again.

"Tricia?"

"Huh?" She stared somewhat blankly at Danielle.

"Orchids?"

"Yeah?"

"So what if it was for some other reason?" Danielle asked. "Like, just to have orchids out there?"

Tricia didn't seem to understand the question. She still had a blank look. Then she seemed to remember that a question had been asked. "Oh, yeah. Well, this is fiction," she said. "In fiction everything has a kind of reason. I thought and thought about it, and realized that the number matched the years. So in the story that's the— Well, it's sort of implied?"

Danielle looked at Judy, then down at the chain and the loop of hair. "You still want to get rid of the hair?"

Judy put her hand to her neck. "No," she said. "I mean if you don't mind. I'd like to keep it."

"I'll make you another," Tricia said. "If you come."

"I'll be there," Danielle said "Look, just take three deep breaths and belt that mother out."

"I'll pee my drawers."

"No you won't. If you can iron the Moloka'i and huli only once, then you can get up and read that story to an audience."

Tricia came out with a shaky sigh. "I just hope—" She stopped, looked at the table again.

"Hope what?"

"I don't know. It's something about the way I wrote it. I don't want any of you to get mad at me."

"Mad?" Donna said. "Why?"

Tricia opened her mouth to speak, but did not. She held her shoulders up in a sustained shrug.

Danielle and Donna exchanged glances. What the hell was she talking about? What could there be in a story that would make anyone mad at her? She looked up at Tricia, who seemed to be looking more at her than anyone else. Then Danielle looked down at the table, a sudden, inexplicable wave of heat flushing her face. What the hell was she up to?

Then she saw her father, Kimo, and Keoni coming across the grass. They were carrying the bags full of all their personal stuff, and her father seemed to be talking somewhat animatedly to Keoni Hong. When they got to the table, they put all the gear down next to the paddles. Then they stood there and looked at the seven of them squeezed around the little table.

"You guys ready to grind?" Kimo asked.

Yeah, sure, whenevers. People began to move around Danielle, and although she wanted to put her head back down on the table, she changed her mind and decided to walk out onto the sand to see the remaining canoes come in, if there were any left.

"I'm gonna go check out the beach," she said.

No one heard. Keoni Hong was talking with the girls he had gone to school with. Lauren, the one who had been sick, said, "Didn't your brother play football?"

"Much older than me," he said.

"No, it's just that I thought—" and then she could not hear the rest.

"—next year," Donna was saying to Danielle's father. "We train all year. If we can come in third, maybe we can come in second, right? By the way, who does your taxes?"

Danielle stepped away from them, adjusted the lei once more, and looked back at the table. Judy and Michelle sat talking, and Danielle watched Judy, wondering about all those years she waited to come out and fix her mess, and she still wasn't ready. Another organism waiting for something, but then she supposed that Judy couldn't be blamed for hesitating at this point. Despite how different they were, they all had to spend part of their lives waiting. And it struck her now how really different they all were, and that, amazingly, all of them in had been in the same canoe. Even Tricia, sitting across from Judy and Michelle and staring at a spot on the table, apparently deep in thought again. About what, nobody knew. Danielle snorted softly and shook her head. "Strange," she said, and walked around the towels and mats toward the ocean. Her walking was shaky and awkward, as if she were learning again how to walk. Her knees were weak, and her feet hurt. She felt airy and washed out, but was familiar enough with the feeling that it didn't bother her. People were still milling around to the right of the jetty, where groups of paddlers were talking, and canoes were being paddled off toward the lagoon end of the beach, where trucks with trailers waited.

She walked along the left side of the jetty so that she could see if any more canoes were coming in, and apparently there were only a couple left, still hundreds of yards away from the buoy, so she walked a little into the water to cool her feet. Standing there, she scanned the horizon, which was now clear, and then looked down at the water lapping on the sand. Near her feet there was movement of some sort, and she shaded her eyes and looked down. There were little silver fish swimming just a couple feet out, darting around in a way that made the sun flash off their sides. They swam in a little school, fanning out and then coming back, then moving in a circle—they stopped, then darted around again, flashing little points of light, and she squinted her eyes a little and saw the fish move around again, and imagined what it must be like for them looking up out of the water, at some huge thing rising from its two pillars planted right there before them and which they were swimming past, the whole school sweeping to a point, seeming to her like a fine veil being pulled through the water.

A resident of Hawai'i since 1966, Ian MacMillan is the author of six novels and four short story collections, one of which won the Associated Writing Programs Award for Short Fiction. He has made over a hundred appearances in literary and commercial magazines, including *Yankee, The Sun, Paris Review, Iowa Review,* and others, and his work has been reprinted in *Best American Short Stories, Pushcart Prize,* and *O. Henry Award* volumes, among other 'best' anthologies. Winner of the 1992 Hawai'i Award for Literature, he teaches fiction writing at the University of Hawai'i. His recent novels include *The Braid* and *The Red Wind* (both set in Hawai'i) from Mutual Publishing, and *Village of a Million Spirits: A Novel of the Treblinka Uprising* from Steerforth Press and Penguin Books (2000), which won the 2000 PEN U.S.A.-West Fiction Award.